BREATHLESS

THE ASPEN SERIES
BOOK TEN

CINDY STARK

OLIVERHEBERBOOKS

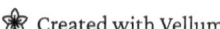 Created with Vellum

1

Laurel Ewing pulled the navy-blue summer sweater over her head and tossed it on the growing pile of discarded clothes on her bed. The remaining clothes in her closet didn't meet her expectations, and she feared she'd find nothing decent to wear.

She should have said no to blind dating. No to *all* dating. Period. "This is pointless."

Afton Searle, best friend extraordinaire, lifted the sweater from the pile and held it up for Laurel to inspect again. "I thought it looked fine."

Laurel rolled her eyes. Afton could make anything look good with her long blond tresses and an enviable figure. With her own auburn hair and fair skin, she had to be a little more discerning. "I don't want *fine*. I want classy. Or sexy. Or how about devastatingly hot?"

She'd never been considered beautiful in the past, by herself or by the guys she knew. Tomboy would be a better description, at least until recently.

Afton sucked her tongue. "You're devastatingly hot in anything you wear."

"You can say that," Laurel tossed over her shoulder, not bothering to look at Afton. "Since you're engaged to a man who adores you. Those of us single ladies worry a bit more."

In fact, the greatest factor in her decision to date for the first time had been her friends' romance. Seeing the happiness Afton had found when she'd fallen in love with the sweet and handsome Corey Kendall left her wanting.

Corey hadn't been another weight in Afton's already heavy load. Instead, he'd helped Afton through some unbearable times, leading Laurel to think she might find a guy to love her like that, too.

Since then, she'd discovered dating wasn't as easy as it looked. Finding someone she might be interested in who was also interested in her had been defeating. "You've forgotten what it's like trudging through the dating swamps, looking for a prince among all the warty, rude, and seriously lacking toads."

Laurel turned and held up a red silk blouse she'd only worn twice. Afton shook her head. "Clashes too much with your hair."

She reined in her frustration and continued the search. There had to be something suitable. "You're not helping."

"Don't worry. You look beautiful just the way you are."

Laurel's irritation slipped out. "Like this? Should I go mostly naked then? Just my bra and panties?"

Afton laughed, bringing a smile to Laurel's face. "You said you wanted to be sexy."

She groaned. "Seriously, though. I do want to make a good impression. You know what they say about first impressions. And don't give me the crap about if he's the right guy, then he'll love me no matter how I look. He's my first actual date that has potential. A successful entrepreneur."

Her friend grinned. "Don't forget hot. And charming."

Laurel snorted at Afton's description. They both knew she was looking for someone strong and steady. Handsome was nice, but unnecessary. "If what you say about him is true, I don't want to blow it."

She wanted to find a guy and get out of the dating pool as fast as possible. No telling how many piranhas swam in those dark and dangerous waters.

Afton curved her lips into a reassuring smile. "He's a great guy. Don't worry. Your only concern tonight is if there's any chemistry. If you pass that critical point, you'll be perfect for each other."

The guy sounded too good to be true. But if he was half the man Afton promised, she could work with that. She didn't need the perfect guy. Just someone she could count on who wouldn't break her heart. As much as she'd tried to convince herself otherwise, she dreaded the thought of being alone forever.

Laurel emptied her lungs with a slow breath. First dates were stressful enough. Blind dates pushed her boundaries of sanity. She wasn't shy. Hell, she'd interviewed tons of people in search of the perfect news or human-interest story. But add in the potential new love interest factor, and her brain went to mush.

"Let me have a look." Afton stepped in front of her closet and rifled through her remaining clothes. "Wear this one."

Laurel had already decided against the forest green button-down blouse. "That won't work. Too plain."

Afton arched a brow. "That's what accessories are for, my dear. Put it on."

She took it with an exasperated sigh. The fabric was soft and had a slight sheen, making it dressier than a plain cotton shirt. She assessed the blouse with fresh eyes as she buttoned it. The color did look good with her hair. "It's not very sexy."

"Undo an extra button. Show a little cleavage. It's not against the law."

No, but it *was* unnatural for her. She slipped the button out of its hole and gave the shirt another opportunity to impress her. She turned to the side and glanced in the mirror. The darts around the midsection tapered the shirt to her curves, and with the one button undone, it hinted at sexy. Subdued sexy.

Afton pointed toward the dresser. "Finish it with that chunky metal heart necklace you have, and I think we have a winner. Perfect for dinner at Pinecone's finest restaurant."

Laurel didn't meet her friend's gaze, but turned to choose her necklace instead. "We're not going to Pinecone. We decided to stick closer to home and meet at Sparrow's." After a long moment of silence, Laurel glanced at her in the mirror.

Afton pinned her with a knowing gaze. "*We decided*? Or you did?"

She flashed a warning look at her friend. "Does it matter? You know I dread going to Pinecone. Plus, if I drive myself, which I wouldn't if we went into Pinecone, I can leave early if things don't work out. Win-win in my book."

Her friend gave her a look that said she was crazy. "If you're both happy with that choice, then I guess that's fine. I would have gone for the nice dinner out of town, but whatever."

Laurel ignored her taunt. "Cowboy boots or heels?"

"I'd go for heels, just to dress it up a bit."

Of course, she would. Afton had tried to persuade her she didn't need to dress to impress, but they both knew she did. For now, she convinced herself that the reward would be worth the effort. All she wanted was a decent guy who could be happy with small town living and a normal, quiet life.

Didn't seem like it was too much to ask.

———

Laurel shifted her old yellow Jeep into park and wiped her sweaty hands on her jeans. *Breathe.* Just breathe, for heaven's sake.

Her heart thudded loudly, fueled by a mixture of excitement and nerves. What if he *was* Mr. Right? What if the man of her dreams waited just inside Sparrow's Bar and Grill? Her odds were fifty-fifty.

It *could* happen.

As she headed toward the door, she scanned the parking lot, looking for a vehicle she didn't recognize. When she found nothing out of the ordinary, she confirmed he hadn't arrived yet.

That was okay. She had shown up a little early because her nerves demanded it. That didn't make him late.

At least she hoped he wouldn't be. That would mean more time to fret about the evening if he was.

Breathe, Laurel.

Fresh air, thick with the scent of pine, helped to lower her anxiety. The evening was beautiful, with the warm summer sun casting its last rays of the day in the western sky. The heat of the day had passed, promising a beautiful mountain night in its wake.

It was the perfect atmosphere for lovers. Maybe, just maybe, she might meet a man she could love, too.

Sparrow's familiar scents of sizzling steaks and beer greeted her as she entered. Several people acknowledged her with a friendly nod. She returned a brief smile before she shifted her gaze from table to table, looking for a tall guy with dark hair, as Afton had described him. Just in case he'd parked elsewhere and was inside, after all.

After checking the front area, she headed toward the back where the music wasn't as loud and several guys played pool.

Her date wasn't there, either. Not that she'd expected him to be.

With her nerves skittering just beneath her skin, she claimed an out-of-the-way seat that faced the front of the bar and focused on calming herself. Becky, the bartender, took her order and returned with a glass of white wine a few minutes later.

Dating sucked. No doubt about it. The entire process was ridiculous. She shouldn't worry about what the guy thought of her. Maybe he should try to impress her instead.

Worse, maybe she'd take one look at him and *not* want him to. Then she'd be left to deal with the sticky chore of extricating herself from the situation without hurting his ego.

Odds were one of them wouldn't be going home happy tonight. Possibly both. Possibly...

A male voice pulled her from her doomsday reverie. "Hey, there."

Laurel lifted her gaze with hope rising in her heart that her date might have arrived, only to have it dashed. Tall, dark, and handsome. One of Corey's friends, if she remembered right. Though she couldn't recall his name. Mostly because she hadn't wanted to remember it.

He was a ladies' man who didn't know how to take no for an answer. At least that's how he'd come across, with his over-the-top flirtations, when she'd briefly met him. And she had no patience for his kind.

She glanced behind him to ensure her date hadn't arrived. The last thing she needed was a good-looking man to scare away her potential soulmate. "Hi," she said, keeping her tone cool.

With midnight eyes and sensuous lips, she could safely assume he'd kicked up plenty of dust on the multitude of broken hearts he'd left as he plowed on to the next. Which was exactly why she'd blown him off more than a year ago on the night Afton had been unjustly arrested.

Laurel never forgot a face. He'd been an outrageous flirt who'd come on far too strong. Knowing how devastating he could be to her wounded psyche, she'd rejected his advances with some well-placed words.

Then everything fell to pieces with Afton's arrest, and she hadn't seen him since. She could have asked Afton's fiancé Corey about him if she'd been interested. But she was smart enough to avoid disaster before the stranger could wreak destruction.

He lifted his chin in an assured manner. "Are you going to tell me your name this time?"

Laurel chuckled as her cheeks heated, surprised that he'd remembered their conversation from that long ago. She gave him the same answer she had back then. "No."

Because if she did, he'd ask for her number next. Then, if he did call, she wouldn't know what to do.

He shook his head. "Still playing hard to get? Doesn't matter. You'll tell me, eventually."

No, she wouldn't.

She glanced behind him again, worried her date would walk in and see them together. Which would not be a great first impression. "I hate to seem rude, but I'm waiting for someone. A date," she added, just in case he didn't catch the hint.

He arched his brows. "Oh, really? Me, too."

She exhaled with relief. He wouldn't be her worry.

He glanced at his watch, and a small frown settled in his expression. "She seems to be running behind. Anyway, nice to see you again."

He gave her a brief nod before he strode away to claim a nearby table, where he could also watch the front door.

She made a face behind his back and then looked away.

Who was he dating anyway? Lexie? Or Mallory? She'd bet it was Mallory with her long, dark hair and pretty, blue eyes. She'd be just his type.

Laurel lifted her glass and sipped to avoid the awkwardness of being alone.

Five minutes passed. Then ten. She grew anxious, wondering if her date had stood her up. Mr. Flirt had caught her sneaking glances far too many times, and she feared he'd think she was lying. She'd consumed more than half the glass of wine she'd ordered, and her evening was on a serious downhill slide.

She heaved a sigh of frustration.

Why did she put herself through this?

Laurel drained the rest of her glass, not wanting to waste the excellent vintage, and stood. Without looking in the flirt's direction, she headed toward the front of the bar. A night at home with the dogs sounded better and better.

"Looks like maybe we've both been ditched," he called out before she got far.

She swiveled on her heels. "Apparently so. That's the last time I let a friend pick a date for me. She promised he was hot, successful, and charming." She might have been bragging, but he deserved it.

His eyebrows shot upward, filling her with satisfaction. "Is that so?" he asked.

Maybe her date had a good reason for not showing, but he could have texted her if he wasn't coming. It was simply rude to leave her waiting with no word. "That's what I was told, but he seems more like a loser to me, and I've waited long enough."

He stood and strode closer before he spoke in a quieter tone. "You're here on a blind date?"

She shrugged, pushing down her embarrassment. "People do that. It's not uncommon, and my friend insisted I should meet this person." It didn't mean that she couldn't get her own dates.

A devilish grin slid across his lips as he shook his head. Then he laughed. "I can't believe it. After all this time, Afton is the one who brought us together."

Laurel gaped at him, thinking there was no way her friend would have hooked them up. Especially not without telling her.

He strode closer, tightening the tension inside her. "She must know you'll have her head after this, though."

Laurel narrowed her gaze in distrust. "What's your name?"

He grinned. "Charlie Blackmore. Is that the name of your date?"

Unfortunately, it was.

If what he said was true, she most certainly would have Afton's head. Laurel's shock shifted to irritation. How could Afton betray her trust like that? She knew Laurel avoided serial flirts like him.

"I can't believe she would set us up without even a warning," Laurel said, shaking her head. "I never would have agreed to this date."

Charlie lifted his hands in a conciliatory gesture, curving his lips into an engaging smile. "Maybe she thought if you got to know me, you'd change your mind. I'm really not that bad."

Maybe he was a decent person. But he wasn't her type.

She met his midnight eyes directly. "I'm sure you're a great guy, but I'm looking for something else. You likely are, too. Enjoy your dinner."

Laurel turned and strode away before he could respond.

2

As Laurel attempted to walk away, Charlie caught her forearm, causing her to halt. "Hang on just a minute."

She controlled her automatic jerk reaction that she'd lived with since her childhood and cautiously extricated her arm from his grasp. "There's no sense wasting your time or mine when I already know this will never work. I'm not your type, and you're not mine."

He tilted his head, his dark eyes drawing her into their depths. "Ah, come on. We've both put effort into getting here tonight, and we both need to eat. We don't have to be each other's types to share a meal, and we can plot how we'll get even with Afton for setting us up."

She supposed he had a point, and it wasn't like her to be rude.

He dipped his head, catching her attention. "Afterward, we'll part ways, maybe even as friends. No harm, no foul." He lifted his brows in a hopeful look that tugged a smile from her.

Maybe he wasn't as pushy and cocky as she'd first thought, and she really didn't want to go home and cook. "Afton *would* deserve it."

His expression brightened. "So, that's a yes?"

Dammit. Most women without her history would just agree and not worry. "Fine. It's a yes."

"Would it be okay to ask your name now?"

She sighed. It would be ridiculous if she didn't tell him. "Laurel Ewing."

He repeated her name, and the grin that curved his lips lit an unwanted spark inside her. She knew without a doubt he was a ladies' man, and she had no intention of getting herself tangled up with that, but damn, he appealed to her feminine instincts. Must be the age-old urge of a woman wanting a man who appeared strong and virile.

Charlie Blackmore was all that and more.

Those qualities were necessary back in the day when a woman's life depended on the man's ability to protect and provide. Times had changed. She could provide for herself. Instead, she searched for a man who could meet her emotional needs, who could understand her past and inspire trust. She wanted to date a good guy, a down-to-earth man who would love her forever.

Messing around with Charlie would be a mistake. If they ended up together, they'd never last. But this was only dinner, she reminded herself.

The feel of his hand on the small of her back as he escorted her toward her table left her tingling where he touched her. Not that she'd admit to anyone, ever, how nice it felt. Still, she wanted a guy to help her navigate the years and trials in life. Someone to love and laugh with. If nothing else, the feelings Charlie inspired reminded her why she'd chosen to pursue marriage.

Two of the town's residents, Nancy and Caroline, paused their conversation to watch with interest as she and Charlie walked past. She knew what that meant. Charlie's innocent touch would surely send the gossiping ladies' tongues a-wagging tomorrow, but she didn't mind.

She was on the market, and it couldn't hurt to have people know.

He helped her into her seat and then claimed the chair across from her. "Afton said I was charming, huh?" he said with a smile.

She snorted as she lifted a menu tucked between a small lamp and the wall, opened it, and then glanced at him. "Actually, I remember thinking you were an obnoxious pain in the ass when we last met."

He placed his palm over his chest as though wounded. "You're hard on a man's ego. Was I that bad?"

His question surprised her. "Uh...yes. You have a way of coming on really strong. It might work for some women, but not me."

He shook his head in defeat. "Damn. You know, it's hard trying to make an impression on a beautiful woman. Should I flirt? Should I hang back? And now I realize she didn't think twice about me the moment she vanished from sight."

Laurel swallowed an uncomfortable lump. He was right. "I may have pushed you from my thoughts, but not for the reasons you're suggesting."

His charcoal shirt darkened his eyes to the color of a forest at night. Deep, mysterious, mesmerizing. A trait that was certain to attract plenty of women who could soothe his ego.

He stared at her and then nodded, as though asking her to continue her thought. "Would you care to enlighten me? It might help me the next time I meet an interesting woman."

She arched her brows. "Are there any women you don't find interesting? At least on a short-term basis."

Charlie leaned back in his chair and frowned. "Wow. Did I really inspire that low of an opinion of me?"

Her compassion kicked in, and she hated that she was being so harsh. It was likely leftover irritation from Afton's betrayal and not his fault. He'd been duped, too.

She cleared her throat. "I'm sorry. It's just that I've met men like you."

He cocked a half-smile. "Men like me?"

She dropped her head into her hand, ashamed of her behavior. When she lifted her gaze, she offered a smile. "I'm sorry. I don't mean to put you down. You have every right to live your life the way you choose. It's just that I'm looking for a monogamous relationship. I don't like playing games, and I'd rather put my energy toward building something."

He stared at her for a long moment and then blinked. "You think I'm a player."

She shrugged, hesitating before she looked him in the eye. "Aren't you?"

He seemed taken aback. "I won't say I haven't dated my share of women, but I won't apologize for it, either."

She'd insulted him. "I only meant that you probably intend to date for some time."

"Until I meet the right person," he countered. "Isn't that what dating is for?"

The way he phrased it made her sound ridiculous. "I meant a guy like you would probably want to date a lot of women first."

He narrowed his gaze, and she knew she'd dug a hole too deep to climb out. "A guy like me? That's twice you've used that label without knowing me."

She sighed. "Never mind. I know I'm not making sense." To herself either. "I probably need to eat. We should order."

The time it took to order and chat about mundane things as they ate put enough distance between their earlier conversation to allow Laurel to relax again. He was more intelligent than she'd given him credit for, but he also caught every lady's eye in the room.

Even so, she had to admit he was a pleasant dinner companion, despite their initial awkwardness. "Afton said you'd recently moved to Aspen. Where did you live before?"

Charlie wiped his mouth with a napkin before leaning back in his chair, studying her with those eyes. "Salt Lake. After I invested with Afton's company, I convinced her to let me open an eclectic restaurant as part of the brewery. Before that, I was in the business sector for several unhappy years, but I've always wanted to be a professional chef."

She widened her eyes. *"You're Afton's partner?"*

He released a soft chuckle. "I have been for a while now. I moved here once she agreed to give the restaurant a go."

Laurel had watched it being built over the past months. Strange that she hadn't run into Charlie when she'd visited Afton there. "That restaurant seems like a huge undertaking."

He laughed. "More so than I'd originally thought. But it's a labor of love."

She admired his drive. "I assume you know your way around the kitchen."

He snorted. "The kitchen and then some."

His not-so-innocent suggestion tightened her insides. "I see."

His eyes flashed with interest, but he only smiled. "Tell me what you do."

She exhaled, grateful for the safe subject. "I majored in English, and now I write for newspapers and magazines. Nothing big for the most part, though I was lucky enough to get an article in Reader's Digest once. Mostly, I'm a regular contributor to the Pinecone Daily. Sometimes one of the Salt Lake papers will pick up my stuff."

He cocked his head. "I've been a pretty avid reader since I've moved to the area, but I don't recall seeing your name."

She lifted her glass and swirled the white wine. "You wouldn't. I use a pen name."

He arched a sexy brow. "Which is...?"

She hesitated for a long moment. The thought of having this man read her work and possibly finding insight into her soul left her feeling vulnerable. "It's a secret."

Mirth brightened his eyes. "You won't tell me?"

He seemed surprised she would deny him, and she dropped her gaze. "Nope."

"Afton will," he countered.

She jerked her attention back to him. "Not if I warn her first."

He held her gaze for what seemed like forever before he nodded and smiled. "You're an interesting woman, Laurel."

Exactly what she didn't want to be to him. Her pen name wouldn't be hard to discover, so she needed a diversion to put those thoughts from his mind. "I have a second job of sorts. I'm the caretaker of Afton's pet rescue foundation. She doesn't pay me, but she lets me live in her grandpa's house rent free in exchange for services."

"Sounds like you have an enjoyable life, doing what you love and hanging out with furry friends. I'm a little envious."

She sent him a confused but happy look. "Why? It sounds like you're doing what you love, too."

He snorted. "I'm just embarking on my journey. You're already successfully supporting yourself with yours. Plus, pets."

A smile blossomed on her lips, and she lifted her glass of wine to hide it. "Do you have fur babies?"

"As a matter of fact." He held her gaze with an unseen force that drew her inexorably closer to him with each passing second. "I adopted Max."

"*Our Max*?" The sweet, adorable Border Collie someone had dumped halfway between Aspen and Pinecone? "I thought Afton gave him to someone out of town...which would be you." She laughed at the crazy number of connections they shared.

"Yep. I was in town a while back to meet with Afton and Corey to discuss my proposal. Afton had Max at the distillery that day, and I fell in love. I took him home with me."

His declaration exhumed bittersweet memories. "I was so sad that I never got to say goodbye to him. He's such a good boy."

"You can come see him anytime you want. I've recently built in that new subdivision in town, so my house isn't too far away. I'm sure he'd love to see you, too."

The thought of going to Charlie's house left her nervous. A person's home was such a personal space, but she adored Max and longed to see him again. "I might do that. I'd really like to see him."

"I could cook for you."

Just like that, they were back in dangerous territory. "That's okay. I wouldn't want you to go to all the trouble."

"It's no trouble. I love to cook. I have some new concoctions and need a test subject."

She swallowed, plotting ways to extricate herself politely, but none came to mind. Her pulse raced faster with each passing second, as though a vicious monster dogged her steps. Why couldn't she leave the past in the past? There was no danger now, she reminded herself once again, fighting to use the tools her psychologist had taught her.

She exhaled a deep breath. "I don't think that's a good idea." Truth and assertiveness.

He seemed genuinely puzzled by her answer. "Why not?"

"Because..." She took a moment to plan her words. "If I let

you cook for me, then that's a date, and we're not dating, remember?"

His eyes flashed with incredulity. "Friends cook for friends all the time. I've had Corey and Afton over on several occasions, and those weren't dates."

"They also weren't single women."

"That's the criteria, then? I can't be friends with any single women? It always has to mean something more?"

"Well...no. Of course not." Funny how she could communicate perfectly with her writing, but spoken words had always been a challenge.

He offered her a warm smile. "How about this, then? May I cook for you as a friend sometime? It would be my pleasure."

This was why she should have left the moment she realized he was her date. "Maybe." She made a point of glancing at her phone to check the time. "I should probably go. I still need to let the dogs out and give them a chance to run around before I put them all to bed."

She thought he would argue with her, but he dipped his head in acknowledgement instead. "Let me pay our bill, and I'll walk you to your car."

"That's unnecessary. We're in small-town Aspen, for heaven's sake, and I'm a capable person."

"That may be, but a gentleman doesn't stop being a gentleman in a small town."

He was right on that account. One reason she'd stayed in Aspen, after she and her mother had moved from Pinecone when she was younger, was that she loved how the town had maintained the societal customs of the past. Though the men here mostly respected women as equals, they treated them like ladies.

If she and the other women wanted that custom to

continue, they had to appreciate the men's gestures. "Thank you, then. That would be nice."

Once again, Charlie placed his hand on the small of her back as they left the restaurant. She focused on relaxing and enjoying his gentle touch, grateful that her rational thoughts didn't completely desert her as they made their way to her Jeep.

He opened her door but caught her hand before she could climb inside.

Charlie peered at her with a sincere gaze. "Thanks for a fun evening. I know it wasn't what you expected, but I enjoyed your company."

Surprising warmth bubbled inside her, but she tamped it down. Though he was even more appealing after they'd shared dinner, she knew his true nature. Her past had taught her to protect herself at all costs. "I did, too."

She meant that. As much as they weren't suited for each other, she did like him, liked to talk to him, and liked how she felt in his presence.

He lifted his brows. "Would it be too much to ask for a hug?"

Could she chance that? Part of her longed to experience something that so many took for granted. Sure, her mom hugged her often, and Afton did too, on many occasions, but this was different. "A friend's hug?" She needed that clarification just to be safe.

"Absolutely." He opened his arms, and she hesitated only a second before she stepped into his embrace.

Incredible warmth surrounded her as he held her against him. She slid her arms around his shoulders, and the intimate contact between their bodies ignited her senses. With her nose close to his neck, she couldn't ignore the woodsy scent of his cologne, nor the way it urged her to take a deeper breath.

He held her for longer than what she was certain friends

hugged, but she had no desire to pull away, either. In her many years on earth, she'd avoided this type of contact with a man, and the power of it left her thoughts jumbled and her knees weak.

Charlie pulled back but didn't release her, and for a quick moment, she feared he'd kiss her.

He didn't, though. He gave her another nod before he stepped back and allowed her room to enter her Jeep. "Thanks again, Laurel, for a memorable evening. Have a good night." He closed her door and strode away before she could respond.

Ah, hell. Now that she'd gotten her wish, and he'd walked away, she ached to call him back, just to hear his voice again. She might see him at Afton's distillery whenever she stopped in, but their intimate dinner had passed.

She'd made her intentions clear, and though they'd agreed to be friends, odds were they'd be nothing more than acquaintances. Which was all they should be.

She started the engine and pulled out onto the quiet street. Several times, she glanced in her rearview mirror to see if she could spot his headlights, but they never came. He must have gone back inside Sparrow's to find someone to fill the rest of his evening.

Later, as Laurel drifted off to sleep that night in her cozy home, she thought of Charlie's embrace, the woodsy scent of his cologne. She touched her arms, remembering the warmth of his. Though she'd made her intentions crystal clear, some deeper part of her wished she hadn't. Wished she was braver. But the fear of being hurt lingered, holding her back.

With a sigh, Laurel rolled over and closed her eyes. She'd done the right thing, even if it left an ache inside. Charlie may intrigue her, but she couldn't let herself get drawn in. Her soul had taken enough for one lifetime.

3

Charlie found Afton toward the back of the distillery, checking her latest batch of whiskey. "Fair warning. You're in a shitload of trouble."

Afton glanced up with a confused frown on her face. "Why is that?"

He leaned against a rack of barrels and folded his arms. "The blind date last night."

She dropped the clipboard and faced him fully. "Did it not go well?"

He snorted. "Depends on your definition of well. I had a pleasant time with a beautiful lady. However..." He held his next words until she furrowed her brows. "It was far from a blind date. We met each other last year on the night Karl arrested you. Remember?"

She widened her eyes. "Oh...that's right. I'd totally forgotten. You'd been in town to see Jerry and Corey. The three of you arrived at Sparrow's at the same time. If I remember right, you threw yourself at Laurel, and she shot you down."

He rolled his eyes. "Thanks for that reminder. I did only slightly better last night. She was ready to walk the moment she saw me. Said she couldn't talk to me because she was waiting for her date. Imagine how excited she was when we realized *I* was her date."

"Oops." She grimaced apologetically. "I'm so sorry. Laurel can be standoffish, though really, she's a very sweet person."

He admonished her with a shake of his head. "Only if she likes you. Which, after some cajoling and a couple of hours in my endearing company, I'm happy to say she doesn't despise me anymore."

"You convinced her to stay for dinner?" Afton seemed surprised. "That's several bonus points right there. I told you that you guys would be good together."

"I'd hardly call us *together*. She let me buy her dinner, but when I asked if I could cook for her, she shot me down again, as you so kindly put it."

Afton considered his words for a few moments. "Well, at least we tried. Can't make the girl do something she doesn't want to, right? You said you had a nice evening, so everything worked out okay in the end."

He fired a look full of derision in her direction. "It did not work out okay. You can bet she has an earful for you, and I..." She remained silent while he worked through his crazy thoughts. "I want to see her again."

A bright grin bloomed on Afton's face. "Really? That's so perfect."

He was an inch from losing his patience with her. "For hell's sake, Afton, it's not perfect. She wants absolutely *nothing* to do with me. She thinks we're completely wrong for each other, and I distinctly got the impression she's not one to change her mind."

Afton gave him a small shrug. "Maybe she just needs her best friend to convince her not to be so rash with her judgements." She smiled, giving him hope. She nodded toward the exit to the office area and started to walk. "I could talk to her."

"No. That won't help. She thinks I'm a womanizer, and she guards her heart well. Even though you know her better than I do, I'd wager if you push, she'll close down even tighter."

In the hallway outside her office, she paused and glanced up at him, her eyes full of caution. "You noticed that, did you?"

"Hard not to." He understood being cautious to avoid heartache, but she hadn't even given him a chance.

"She had...a...it's complicated." Afton couldn't spill Laurel's childhood trauma. "Just don't hold it completely against her. She's the best person I know. She is looking for a great guy to date, and I can't think of anyone better than you."

He snorted, but appreciated her sentiment. "I guess one vote of confidence is better than none."

"*Afton?*"

The sound of Laurel's voice coming from the lobby stopped them both and brought their gazes sharply together.

Charlie glanced toward the distillery and then back at Afton. "You'd best tackle this one alone."

"You're leaving me? But it's another opportunity to see Laurel."

"It's not in my best interest or yours this time around. Good luck, partner." He grinned as she cursed softly and headed for the reception area. Halfway there, he realized he'd forgotten to ask Laurel's pen name. After Laurel had her chance with Afton, it would be too late.

Without waiting to hear any fireworks, he strode into the operations area and ducked out a side door. Laurel would tell Afton what she needed to, and his presence would only complicate matters.

———

Laurel marched around the corner of the dark gray marble reception desk but stopped short when she caught sight of Afton heading her way.

Her friend pasted on a bright smile. "Good morning. I just made coffee. Would you like some?"

She had no patience for niceties. "What I want is to talk. I seriously thought about calling you last night to give you a piece of my mind, but then I decided I'd rather look you in the eye when I called you a liar and a conniver."

"Ouch." Afton grimaced. "I'm so sorry, Laurel. Charlie told me what happened. I swear on my life I didn't remember that you guys had met before. You know how crazy that night was for me. Please. You have to believe me."

The sincerity in her eyes urged her to forgive her friend, but she needed Afton to understand. She'd thought Afton knew her parameters for dating, but obviously, she didn't. Damn Abercrombie for putting them there in the first place.

"There was a reason I turned down Charlie the first time we met. He's a player, a heartbreaker. You know my issues, and you know I'm not up for that kind of relationship. Why would you *ever* think we would be good together?"

Afton's expression turned perplexed. "Charlie is one of the nicest guys I know, Laurel. I'm not sure where you get this idea that he's a player, and I would hope you'd know I always have your best interests at heart."

Sometimes Afton could be so blind. "Do you really think a guy that handsome is going to settle for a woman before he's tasted them all? If someone gave you a box of chocolates and you didn't know what was inside each one, but you could have as many as you wanted, would you stop at just one?"

Afton snorted. "Chocolates are vastly different from women."

She threw her hands up in frustration. "I don't see that. I

see a guy who could have his pick of the ladies. He's going to play. You remember the way he hit on me the first time? I told you before. I need someone who's solid and steady. Someone I can trust. If I'm going to do this dating thing, I need to be safe."

"You're saying you can't trust him based solely on his looks? Do you realize how ludicrous that sounds?"

Laurel folded her arms in front of her. "Ludicrous or not, I know what I know, and I won't put myself in that position. You know my reasons."

"I know your mom plays on your fears and makes you worry more than you should."

She couldn't deny it, but she wasn't going to admit to anything right now. Her reasons remained unchanged. "This has nothing to do with my mom. Just because she overly worries, doesn't mean her points aren't valid. I set my own conditions."

A brief look of defeat crossed Afton's features, but she quickly replaced it with determination and pointed a finger at Laurel. "I seem to recall a certain someone asking me why I thought I was so special that I wouldn't have to risk my heart like everyone else. I'd like to formally toss that back at you."

"That's not fair. You and I don't have the same background." She'd worked hard to accept what had happened to her and did her best to work around it. "I'm not saying love won't be a risk, but I need to mitigate possible heartbreaks. If I only date down-to-earth, good-hearted men, then I greatly improve my chances."

Afton snorted at that, and Laurel frowned. "If only we could all judge a book by its cover and be correct."

"I'm not naïve, Afton. I know what's at stake here. After all this time of hiding from life, I'm finally ready to step forward. But I sure as hell am not walking straight into the lion's den."

"He's not a lion, Laurel. Sure, he's cute, and he can be a bit flirty."

A bit?

"But he's a good man, and I think you're mistaken." She sent her a pointed look. "He likes you, you know?"

A sharp pang of yearning pierced her and momentarily stole her breath. For too long, she'd ignored the ache in her heart, and it left her dangerously vulnerable. She held out for a few seconds before curiosity defeated her. "What did he say?"

"Just that he had a great time, that he thinks you're a lovely lady, and he'd like to see you again."

Her heart took notice, but fear quickly jumped in. She *could* take a chance with him, her heart argued, but she'd have to give up all illusions of security if she did. "That won't happen, so you'd both better get used to the idea. I'm not saying he's not a good person, okay? And God knows, he's attractive, but he's not the right one for me. Understand?"

Afton sighed. "I do, Laurel. I'm not trying to hound you. You've made some tremendous efforts to reclaim your life, and I'm only trying to support you with a little push. But you believe what you believe, and nothing is going to change that. You know your heart better than anyone."

Finally. "Thank you."

Afton lifted hopeful brows. "The offer for coffee's still open."

"I can't stay. I'm on deadline for an article for the paper. I need to turn it in by noon."

"Okay, then breakfast tomorrow at Rumors? You know you can't resist their warm, sticky cinnamon rolls."

"Sure. That sounds good." Despite being miffed at Afton's screw-up, she treasured their steadfast friendship. And she appreciated that they could discuss anything openly without jeopardizing that rock-solid base. "One more thing."

"What's that?"

"Don't tell him my pen name."

Afton shook her head in disappointment. "I won't ask why."

Together, they walked to the entrance, where Afton gave her a hug before sending her out into the morning sunshine.

Laurel strode across the cobblestone walkway toward her Jeep, replaying their conversation. Afton had meant well, but Laurel had to trust her gut. She needed safe and dependable, not sexy and charming.

From the corner of her eye, she caught a movement and glanced in that direction. *Charlie*. Her heart stopped, along with her footsteps. He hadn't noticed her.

He carried a large cardboard box on his shoulder, heading from a smaller outbuilding toward the operations part of the main building. The man moved with a powerful predatory smoothness, strong and determined. His biceps bulged from the weight of his load, and for one long, luscious moment, she allowed her basic instincts to take over.

He liked her, wanted to spend more time with her. Who wouldn't be flattered by that?

Her body begged her to answer his call. But deep in her heart, she knew falling for him would be like eating that entire box of chocolates. Divine deliciousness for a few moments, followed by endless, self-loathing regret. Her counselor had cautioned her to avoid those types of extremes, and that's what she intended to do.

Without warning, he paused halfway between the buildings and looked around. He stopped when his gaze connected with hers. A swift curl of addictive excitement whipped through her, reminding her of the first time she'd jumped out of a plane.

For a long moment, he stared. Her heart thundered, but she couldn't move.

Then he dipped his head in acknowledgement and continued on his way.

He liked her, but he also seemed to respect her decision.

Good.

Life would be simpler this way.

4

Charlie secured his gloved hands around his end of a walnut dining table meant to seat six and glanced at Afton's fiancé and his long-time partner-in-crime. "Got your end?"

"Yep," Corey Kendall responded and together they carried the table into the restaurant at Sagecreek. "I hear you crashed and burned the other night on your date with Laurel."

Charlie shifted the extra weight to Corey's end and grinned at his groan that followed. "Your wife should be careful what she says."

Corey had been one of his best friends for years and the whole reason he was into this endeavor with Afton now. Charlie knew Corey teased him like guys would, but Laurel's rejection still stung.

He knew he was lucky that he'd only been dumped once before, but this was the first time he'd been flat out turned down before he'd had the chance to charm the lady.

Corey lifted his end higher, redistributing the weight. "Can't blame Afton for telling the truth."

Charlie eyed him. "Wanna bet? I'm going to call her Old Lady Smith if she keeps talking about everyone's business."

Corey snorted. "Don't worry, buddy. She's only telling me because she cares about both of you."

He knew that, too, but still...

They set the table down. Corey strode forward and clapped him on the back. "It's for the best, anyway. She's not right for you."

That was exactly what he *didn't* want to hear. "Really? Afton seems to think we're perfect for each other."

"That's because Afton wants the world to be perfect. She's looking at things through her lens and not Laurel's."

Why would her look on life be so different from Afton's? "Laurel's lens. What does that mean?"

Corey's eyes widened ever so briefly. "Is this where you want it?"

Several long seconds passed as Charlie stared at him. The air between them thickened by degrees. "That doesn't answer my question."

Corey cleared his throat. "Everyone is different, you know? We all think differently." He headed outside to unload more furniture, and Charlie hurried to catch up. He wasn't about to let things go that easily.

Charlie grabbed the end of another table but didn't lift. "She's a hard lady to get to know. After an hour of conversation, I didn't learn much more than that she lives at Afton's old house and that her mom also lives in town."

"Both true. She moved here from Pinecone when she was eleven."

Charlie narrowed his eyes. "You remember, or she told you?"

Corey gave him a dismissive shrug. "I remember because it was the first time my dad let me go to the Fourth of July derby, and Laurel was there. She and her mom had moved to town some months before, but it was the first time I saw her."

"She wasn't at school?" Aspen would be a hard place to go unnoticed for several months.

He furrowed his brows. "Her mom homeschooled her until the next fall, if I remember right."

It might not be much, but at least Corey had given him some information. "Is her dad out of the picture, then?"

"Must be. I've never asked, but I don't think he's ever come to Aspen. And neither her nor her mom have ever mentioned him. It's kind of like he never existed."

"Interesting." Charlie snorted. "I've learned more about her in five minutes than I did with her all night. I wish she wasn't so closed down."

"Well, it's like I said. You're better off looking elsewhere. Afton says she has a particular type of guy in mind, and apparently, you're not it."

That was bullshit. How did she know what kind of guy he was? No one knew the real him. The truth was, Laurel couldn't make a fair judgment until they'd had a proper chance to date, and he needed to figure out a way to make that happen.

Corey narrowed his gaze as though he knew where Charlie's thoughts had drifted. "Look, man. She's a quiet, reserved sort. You're more outgoing. You like to do crazy shit like getting super drunk and then go bungee-jumping."

Charlie shot him an annoyed look. "That was years ago."

"She likes to be at home unless she's..." He shook his head. "Trust me. You wouldn't make each other happy."

"Unless she's what?" he prompted.

Corey released a deep sigh. "Unless she's skydiving so she can write about it."

He barked a laugh. Her human-interest stories were for

adventurers? "Seriously? That's amazing. What name does she write under?"

"Doesn't matter, man. You're not what she's looking for."

"Screw that." Charlie dismissed his comment with a shake of his head. They had more in common than she realized. He was done with this line of negative conversation, and he lifted his end of the table. "Let's go."

After they placed the second table, he turned toward the exit, irritated with Afton, with Corey, and pretty much everything right now. He might be frustrated with himself most of all because he seemed powerless to forget her. He hated when people judged others, and most especially when they judged him.

He'd had enough of that growing up with his overbearing father telling him who was good enough to be his friend, and who was a waste of time and would keep him from achieving his goals. Like his dad had any actual idea of Charlie's goals or intentions about life.

His father had lost his cool when Charlie had told him about leaving the family's mega corporation to invest his time and talents in the distillery and restaurant instead. He'd even threatened to cut him off.

Like Charlie cared.

He'd made his home here in Aspen, and it would be a good one. He'd do what he had to make the eatery a success, and by God, he'd find a way to convince Laurel to give him one more chance.

———

It took three weeks before Laurel found a reason to return to the distillery. She would have stayed away longer, but Afton had summoned her to discuss their pet shelter venture and made all kinds of excuses why they couldn't meet at the house. Afton argued she was too busy with planning wedding details and the opening of the restaurant at Sagecreek Whiskey.

Since Afton was the one who'd gotten their shelter off the ground and allowed her to stay at her grandfather's old farm rent-free, Laurel figured she owed it to her to do whatever it took to make the shelter a success. Not only out of loyalty, but because she deeply cared about all their rescue animals, too.

Still, she wondered if it was a ploy to get her and Charlie together again.

A flash of disappointment nicked Laurel when she didn't see Charlie's silver Dodge parked alongside the distillery, like it had been the last time she'd visited. It wasn't that she wanted to see him. Okay, she did, but only from a distance. Time hadn't dimmed her interest in him, nor had it dimmed her reasons to stay away.

Resetting her thoughts to business, she made her way toward Afton's office and poked her head inside to ensure all was clear.

Afton smiled brightly when she caught sight of Laurel. Her eyes grew even bigger when she spied the white bakery sack from Rumors. "Sweet mercy. You brought cinnamon rolls. I could kiss you."

"I figured I'd better after I canceled our last breakfast date." She hadn't wanted to disappoint her friend, but she'd needed more time to process her date with Charlie before Afton influenced her again.

Afton stood and held out her hand. "Apology accepted."

Laurel snorted. They'd shared many of life's difficulties over Rumors' incredible cinnamon rolls.

Afton took a big bite. "I have some good news and some bad news," she said around a mouthful.

"What's that?" Laurel said, having the same issues enunciating properly.

Afton visibly swallowed and chased it with coffee. "Good news. Marybeth in Pinecone scored a large haul of dog food for free. A few months back, Marybeth joined a pet non-profit group and heard about its availability. When a certain company overproduces and doesn't have storage space, they donate it to this group. Marybeth asked for enough for both our shelters."

"That's incredible, and we have tons of space to store it in the barn."

"The bad news...well, there are two parts, possibly three parts of bad news."

Laurel frowned. "You can't make my day and then turn around and destroy it two seconds later. I deserve a little time to be happy first."

"Sorry." She took another bite of cinnamon roll before she spoke again. "Let's get back to the matter at hand. First part of the bad news is that, although we're gaining dog food, our grant money will be reduced next year. They're cutting back, which we knew could happen."

Oh, damn. "At least we have the kibble."

Afton agreed. "If we keep that attitude, we'll be fine. Corey and I spoke, and we're both willing to add extra personal funds if needed."

"Same. Whatever we need to do. Our work is important. Maybe we could do a fundraiser."

Afton licked the frosting off her finger. "Great idea. Let's plan that after my wedding. Continuing on. If we want the dog food, we need to pick it up. It's sitting in front of Marybeth's house, baking in the sun, so we need to get it today. I have a conference call at one with a potential new investor, so I can't go."

Laurel shrugged. "I don't mind going. It will give me a

chance to review my ideas for my latest article on the benefits of hiking alone in the mountains, and then I can write it later tonight."

Afton's gaze turned questioning. "Explain to me how a woman who's brave enough to spend a week in the wilderness alone where there are bears and wolves is afraid to date a perfectly acceptable man."

She lifted her hands in frustration. "I'm messed up, okay? I can't help who I am and how I feel. Why are you so set on Charlie and keep pushing him on me?"

"I'm not pushing."

"You're not?" They both knew that was nonsense.

Afton dropped her shoulders and gave a guilty grin. "Maybe just a little, but it's because I see something in him that you might, too, if you'd give him a chance."

Laurel cleared her throat. "I'll try to explain. Bears and wolves are predictable, unless, of course, they're hurt. I'm able to learn the dangers of the wild and avoid them. People are not the same. Someone who looks perfectly acceptable could be a wolf in disguise. By the time I figure that out, it would be too late. See the difference?"

Her friend gave her a sad smile. "I see, and I would agree with you if I didn't know Charlie, but I do. I know him well enough to know he's not a danger to you."

She puffed her cheeks with air and expelled a frustrated breath. "I wish I had more time to argue with you, but I need to pick up the kibble. If there's a problem, I'll let you know. Otherwise, I'll take it straight to my house and unload it."

Afton snorted. "The amount of dog food you'll be picking up won't fit in your Jeep. We're talking about a couple of pallets' worth."

Driving Afton's old truck would make the trek less pleasant, but she'd already agreed to the task. "Fine. I'll take your beast."

"Small problem. I don't trust my old truck to haul that much weight without breaking down."

Annoyed, Laurel turned to face her friend directly. Afton was usually much more organized. The stress of wedding plans and the restaurant's grand opening must have gotten to her. "Then how will we get it? Corey's truck?"

"Corey's in Salt Lake for some legislative thing and won't be home until tomorrow."

"Great. Who's going with me?" Laurel asked.

Afton bit her lip, giving Laurel a sheepish look. "Well, I asked Luke, but he's out of town..."

Laurel nodded, mentally running through a list of potential volunteers. "What about Milo? Or Tyler from the feed store?"

"They weren't available today either." Afton cleared her throat. "But I did find someone who can help."

Dread crept up Laurel's spine at Afton's hesitant tone. She had a sinking suspicion she knew exactly who her sly friend had recruited.

Afton's expression changed into a hopeful look. "Charlie."

Laurel stared in disbelief. "Oh, hell."

5

"You can't be serious about sending Charlie with me." The words exploded from Laurel's mouth before she could think straight.

Afton looked wounded. "Why not? He's agreeable."

Her friend had to be out of her ever-loving mind. "I'm not going to let you manipulate me like this. There's no reason Charlie can't go on his own. He can get the grant materials, or Marybeth can mail them to us. You can ask questions over the phone after you review. I'd even be happy to review what she sends and fill out the grants for you."

"Except Charlie needs someone to show him where Marybeth lives."

Was she serious? The man didn't appear to be an idiot. "I'm sure his phone has GPS, or he can print out a map before he leaves. I'll even do that for him."

Afton's face softened into sadness. "Please, Laurel. I promise this isn't a setup. I would totally go if I could. I feel like our shelter needs representation there, and you'll show Marybeth the right amount of genuine gratitude. Charlie would try, of course, but it's not the same. Marybeth is willing to sit down with one of us and go over the details of the grants. It's our best chance to get more funding. You know as well as I do that if we don't keep the money flowing in, we won't be able to help all the sweet kitties and doggies who need us."

Laurel groaned inwardly as the wheels of friendship and duty flattened her like a steamroller. "Nothing like laying it on thick."

Afton gave her a quick nod. "I'll admit I am, but only because I need you so much."

She stalled as she searched for another excuse, but her creative mind left her high and dry. "Fine. I'll do this for you and for the shelter, but you'd better not be playing cupid."

Laurel mentally calculated the time it would take to drive to Pinecone, have Charlie load supplies while she met with Marybeth, and then drive home. A good ninety minutes for sure.

She'd managed to hold her composure for more than an hour over dinner on their first date, her heart reminded her. Not only that, but she'd enjoyed most of their conversation. Maybe she could manage this, too.

Also, Charlie *was* well-aware of her decision not to date and despite his original enthusiasm, he didn't seem like the kind of guy to force himself on her.

Damn.

Millions of butterflies danced in her stomach. Still, that was no reason to be a coward and leave her best friend and unknown pets to suffer the consequences.

She exhaled a heavy sigh. "When do we go?"

Afton's genuine smile touched her heart. "He's ready whenever you are. You can find him back in the new kitchen area. A bunch of supplies arrived this morning, and he's unpacking until you're ready."

So, that's where he'd parked his truck. "What if I would have said no?"

Happiness glowed in her eyes. "I knew you wouldn't let me down."

What could she say to that? Afton had watched her back so many times over the years. Laurel would always do the same.

She steeled her nerves as she headed out a side door toward the restaurant's courtyard. As she walked, her palms grew damp at the thought of seeing Charlie again.

Inside, she called out as she headed for the kitchen. "Hello?" Scents of fresh wood and paint tickled her nose, and she inhaled deeply, loving the smells.

When she entered the kitchen, Charlie turned, surprise flashing in his beautiful dark eyes. A smile spread across his face. "Hey. How have you been?"

Many people said those exact words as a way of greeting, but she had the distinct impression Charlie meant them. "I'm good. Work and animals keep me busy."

"I bet. But a good kind of busy, right?"

Her eyes drifted to the Harley emblem on his t-shirt and the way it fitted to his pecs, but grew looser toward his waist. She realized where her thoughts had drifted, and she mentally scolded herself. She was here for the shelter, not to ogle Charlie.

Clearing her throat, she gestured at the unfinished space. "Yes, very busy. Much like you appear to be here." She glanced about the room, giving her overactive attraction a break. "It will look beautiful when it's done. Very cozy."

She winced internally at the inane comment. Charlie nodded, launching into his plans to attract patrons to avoid becoming a business who failed during the first year. Laurel tried to focus as he spoke, but his nearness made her skin tingle uncomfortably.

"Laurel," he said, catching her attention.

She widened her eyes. "I'm sorry. What?"

He studied her with an unreadable expression. "Do you

have suggestions that would help me avoid becoming a statistic?"

Lauren nodded slowly as the cogs in her mind kicked in. "Obviously, Aspen residents will come unless your cooking totally sucks."

He grinned. "It doesn't."

She smiled at his quick comeback. "But I would think you'd want to entice people from Pinecone to come as well, which means you'll need to make it a destination."

He pointed a finger at her. "Exactly. Good food, along with an atmospheric experience they won't forget."

"I would say it's not impossible to succeed here. But it's definitely riskier than opening the same restaurant in downtown Salt Lake where you have a large population of people to support it."

Charlie cocked his head. "Gotta take a risk every once in a while, Laurel. Can't follow your dreams if you don't, and life will become stagnant."

She knew what he was hinting at, but he didn't understand her history. "Stability is a good thing. Studies show people live longer with less stress in their lives."

He tilted his head and studied her. "I'll counter that with what's the use of being alive if you're not living?"

Her mind stalled, and she blinked several times to restart it. "You know what I mean."

He set the wineglass on the counter next to several others and joined her on the opposite side. "No, I really don't. I was miserable working a predictable job from nine to five, Monday through Friday. I crave new experiences and seeing new places, discovering more about our world."

She caught a hint of his cologne and had to work to keep her thoughts straight. Vibrant energy radiated off him and messed with her head more than she'd expected. She tilted her face upward to look him in the eye. "There's nothing wrong with a quiet life behind a white picket fence."

"I suppose not as long as you get away from time to time to have fun." His gaze pierced hers. "What do you do for fun, Laurel?"

She swallowed. "Stuff."

"Stuff?"

She nodded, her thoughts completely off-rail now.

"Hmm..." A cryptic smile crossed his lips. "We should probably hit the road, don't you think? I'm sure it will take us a couple of hours to get it done."

His question jerked her out of her haze. Had he been calculating the time together as well? He hadn't outright flirted with her like he'd done the other times they'd been together. Was he over his attraction to her so soon and on to another woman?

She wouldn't be surprised. Shouldn't be disappointed. Men like him were prone to that, especially if a woman didn't show interest. With so many to choose from, why pick a difficult target?

She could be damn glad she'd followed her intuition and hadn't fallen for his seductive eyes and honeyed words like many before her probably had. "Lead the way."

He headed for the exit, pausing to hold the door for her. As Laurel brushed past him, his warm scent surrounded her.

She clenched her fists and marched toward his truck. Fine, he still affected her, but it changed nothing. This trip didn't have to mean anything at all.

6

Charlie's late model Dodge truck shone like polished silver in the sunlight. Laurel reached to open her own door, but Charlie's hand was on the handle before she had a chance. His fingers brushed her skin as he took her elbow to assist her into his truck. His touch resulted in a million skitters of electricity running across her nerve-endings, lighting her up much like the glittering lights of Las Vegas.

"Thank you," she offered as she settled herself in his truck.

A moment later, he climbed into the driver's seat and started the engine. She soon realized his ride was far preferable to hers and beat the hell out of Afton's old beast.

Polite conversation about the weather, townsfolk, and his dog filled most of the twenty-minute ride there. Even when silence descended over the cab of the truck for a few moments, she didn't experience the awkward pressure to fill the void like she did with many people. When one could ignore the player in him, which Laurel could, because she wasn't dating him, she could understand why Afton liked him so much.

They'd reached Pinecone's city limits when Charlie tapped his brakes. "Son of a bitch," he hissed.

Laurel shot a glance into the rearview mirror. Red and blue flashing lights rapidly approached from behind. "Were you speeding?"

He flashed a frustrated glanced in her direction. "Hell, I don't know. Probably."

Charlie pulled to the side of the road, and Laurel bit her bottom lip. She'd never been fond of law enforcement. No fault of their own. She appreciated their service immensely. But she'd never completely succeeded in separating the horrific experience of her youth from the men who'd come to her rescue. At the time, every sensory detail had strung together in a tangled mess with people yelling, lights blaring, and her shaking uncontrollably down to her core.

Big, buff Deputy Karl Gardiner, with a god complex, emerged from his police cruiser and her grimace deepened. "Be careful," she said in a low voice. "He can be a real asshole."

"Great." Charlie lowered his window as the officer approached.

"Going a bit over the speed limit, Lead Foot. I'll need to see your license and registration."

"Of course." Charlie shot her a quick glance as he reached for the glove box in front of her. He pulled out a stack of papers, but none readily looked like his registration.

"Would you like me to help?" she offered, hoping to ease his tension. "I can go through those while you get your license from your wallet."

He set the stack on her lap. "Sure. Thanks."

Karl tilted his head to peer inside at her. "Well, if it ain't Laurel Ewing."

Laurel narrowed her gaze at the cocky deputy, tamping down her fear of authority figures. "Hello, Karl."

"Haven't seen you in Pinecone for years. Thought you'd sworn off the place after—"

"Yes," she said, purposefully cutting him off. "It's been a while. Charlie and I are here to pick up donated dog food for the Aspen shelter."

He studied her with a look that left her uneasy. "Is that right?"

She gave him a brief nod and then focused on the paperwork in her lap. The sooner she found Charlie's registration, the sooner they could leave. That's all that mattered.

Laurel still didn't understand why Karl hadn't lost his job along with his uncle, the former mayor of Aspen, the previous year. Karl had unlawfully taken Afton into custody on his uncle's orders and hauled her to jail. Afton had explained that Karl had only been a pawn in the game his uncle played to punish her beloved grandfather.

Maybe so, but she wouldn't have let Karl off the hook so easily. Or at least she hoped she wouldn't. As a youngster, she wanted nothing more than to hide from all the gossip and speculation. Perhaps Afton felt the same. She certainly had more important things to worry about these days, like her new business and her upcoming wedding.

Laurel's heart leapt for joy when she unfolded Charlie's registration. "Here." She thrust the paper toward Charlie, and he presented it along with his license to the annoying deputy.

Karl briefly nodded at them. "I'll be right back."

Silence descended, and Laurel bit her lip again. "I'm so sorry. This is my fault."

He kept his gaze trained on his rearview mirror. "It's not your fault. I'm the idiot who was speeding."

Guilty feelings weighed heavily on her. "I know, but you wouldn't be here if we hadn't asked for your help."

He turned to her then, his engaging eyes pulling her in once again. "It's no big deal. If he gives me a ticket, it will be my first. My record is clean, so it won't affect my insurance."

She widened her eyes. "You've *never* had a speeding ticket before?"

"Don't seem so shocked. I know how to follow the rules... most of the time."

She leaned back against the seat and folded her arms as a small smile tickled her lips. "Sounds to me like you're the one who's living a boring life."

Karl returned, cutting off any further discussion. "I'm citing you for driving nine over the speed limit, although I clocked you at twelve."

"Thank you, sir." Charlie did seem properly contrite.

"Sign here. Your signature does not constitute admitting guilt should you decide to fight this in court."

Charlie scrawled his signature along the bottom of the citation. "I'm not going to fight it. I've learned my lesson."

"Good." Karl handed a copy of the ticket to him. "Keep to the speed limit and have a nice day."

The deputy glanced past Charlie, making it a point to catch Laurel's gaze. "Don't be a stranger. I doubt anyone in town even remembers." He patted the side of Charlie's truck and strode back to his vehicle like the cocky son of a bitch that he was.

Charlie turned to her with a quizzical look. "What don't they remember?"

Panic gripped her insides, but she refused to look away and give him more fodder for his curiosity. "Nothing. Just something embarrassing that happened back in high school." It was the best she could come up with.

He hesitated, keeping his eyes trained on her. "You're not going to tell me?"

She snorted. "No." Telling this man about her past—no. Telling *anyone* about those tragic events would not happen. Those demons would stay locked where they belonged. The sooner she and Charlie accomplished their task and headed out of this godforsaken town, the better. Because she knew plenty of people around who would never forget that day.

He waited a second more and then put the truck into drive. "You're no fun."

"Really, it's nothing. I just prefer to leave it in the past where it belongs."

"I understand. It's kind of like when I went streaking through a Fourth of July parade with nothing on but a Halloween mask."

"*You what?*"

"Just kidding." His smile hooked her deep inside. "I thought maybe it would make you feel better."

Fact was, he had. She rolled her eyes and shook her head, but her lightened mood remained. "Just drive."

He found Marybeth's house with no help from her, which made Laurel wonder again if she'd fallen for a ploy to get them alone together. Two pallets of bagged dog food sat along the edge of the road in front of Marybeth's house, just like Afton had promised.

"I don't know why Afton thought I needed help." He maneuvered his truck, backing until the bed nearly bumped the stacked pallets. "I found my way here just fine."

So, the ploy was all on Afton, and now she felt like she needed to explain her presence so that Charlie didn't think she'd had anything to do with the setup, either. "Marybeth has the grant information for me." Except now that she'd given her reasons, she wondered if that made her seem guiltier.

He inclined his head. "Ah. I see."

She smiled briefly to cover her awkwardness and then hopped out of his truck before he could get her door again. She appreciated his chivalry, but the inside of the truck had suddenly grown uncomfortable, and she needed space. "I'll hurry so I can help you load."

"No worries. You take care of what you need to."

She strode through the sweltering summer heat as confidently as she could to Marybeth's cheery yellow door, feeling his gaze searing her the entire time. When she glanced back, she found him solely focused on his task, and she frowned.

He *had* lost interest in her.

Laurel rang the doorbell, and her smile returned when bright and bustling Marybeth opened the door. The woman had a good twenty years on Laurel, but her engaging vitality and enthusiasm would argue otherwise.

"Well, hello, Laurel. I'm happy to see you. Please come in." She glanced behind Laurel before she closed the door. "Looks like you brought a strapping man to help. Can't say I mind the man-candy."

Laurel laughed at her bold honesty as she appreciated the air conditioning inside the house. "He looks like he can handle the job, right?"

"I'll say." She led her farther into the living room.

Laurel lifted an overstuffed turquoise pillow from the brown suede couch and sat. From her vantage point, she had the perfect view, and it took her breath away. Charlie lifted each bag as though it weighed nothing and tossed it into the back of his truck.

"He's Afton's business partner, right?"

"Mm-hmm." His biceps worked and bunched in a delicious display of muscle and sinew that left her brain fuzzy.

A hand on her elbow brought her back to reality.

"He really is something to look at, isn't he?" Marybeth asked.

Laurel swiveled her gaze to the pile of information Marybeth had sat between them, embarrassed she'd been caught staring. She lifted the first grant application. "Afton said you have some good prospects for grants."

Marybeth frowned. "They're not going to be anything great like what we've had. We'll be catching a chunk of change from here and there. Despite that, anything is better than nothing."

"Agreed. It's hard to picture having to turn away any pet in need. I couldn't do it. I think I'd starve before I'd let them put one down just because it had no one to love it."

"You're a good woman, Laurel. Okay, let's get to these. I hate to rush, but I'm dropping off a potential adoptee at two. I didn't get the best vibe from the woman who wants him, so I'd like to get a look at her place and the shape of her other dog before I hand over one of mine."

More than thirty minutes later, Marybeth sent her back outside with a cold bottle of soda in her hand. Charlie wiped his brow with his forearm and smiled. The hair along his forehead was damp from exertion, and his chest expanded with deeper breaths.

She held out the offering. "Marybeth sent this for you."

"Much appreciated." He took several long swallows and then set it on the tailgate. "I should be finished in a few minutes."

He hefted another bag into the back of the mostly full truck with a grunt. "It's pretty warm out. If you'd like to crank up the air conditioning in the truck, you can."

She glanced at the remaining stack. "I can help."

"They're heavy. Especially after you've lifted a few."

She heaved one into her arms. "I'm not a wimp." She staggered a second before he rescued her.

He turned and tossed it into the truck bed. "Never said you were."

He made it look so easy. She grimaced and met his gaze. "But I obviously don't have muscles like yours."

The grin that slid so easily onto his lips tightened her insides. "Do you want muscles like mine?"

Not to own. But maybe to touch. "No."

"I'm sure there are plenty of other things you do better than me. Like write."

"I guess." She wanted to be helpful, but she couldn't. Instead, she appreciated how nice it was to have him do the heavy lifting for her. However, her conscience wouldn't allow her to sit in an air-conditioned truck while he worked. "How many bags do you think are here?"

"Thirty-five on the first pallet, so about seventy total."

"Wow. At forty pounds each?" She mentally calculated the total, gasping a little inside as she did. "By the time you're done, you will have lifted twenty-eight hundred pounds. That's over a ton."

He chuckled, his breath coming hard. "Trust me. I'm feeling it."

She and Afton had asked too much of one man. "Then you'll have to turn around and unload it at my house?"

He paused, rested an elbow on the edge of the truck's bed, and trapped her with an electric gaze. "Are you saying I'm not up to it?"

Not even. He so obviously was. "I'm saying that we've asked an awful lot of you."

A hint of a grin tickled the corners of his lips. "Then you're saying you'd like to make it up to me by...say, cooking dinner for me?"

Being a single mom, her mama had relied on help from many over the years. One thing she'd ingrained deeply into her was that you always showed gratitude to those who'd helped you. Laurel worried he might take her invitation the wrong way, but whatever attraction lingered seemed to be one-sided on her part. "Of course. Thank you so much for helping our shelter. I would be happy to feed you."

His brows arched toward his hairline in surprise. The grin

that followed burrowed straight into her heart. "Excellent. What are you cooking?"

His question caught her off-guard, and she rushed through a series of thoughts that ended in the fact she'd just offered to cook for a professional chef. "On second thought, how about if I buy you dinner?"

His expression turned to disappointment. "It's not the same as a home-cooked meal."

Nerves twisted like aggressive vines inside her, leaving her anxious. "I know, but I'd forgotten you were an amazing cook when I offered. If you compare my cooking to yours, you're going to wish we'd eaten out. Seriously, I can't cook a decent grilled cheese. Let me save you the trouble and suffering."

"I'm sure you're a great cook."

Not even close. She exhaled as desperation set in. "We could even eat here in Pinecone. I'll buy you a nice steak. After all this work, you deserve it."

He tilted his head and intensified his gaze. "I thought you disliked dining in Pinecone."

Oh...oops. She'd forgotten she'd used that excuse. Fact was, the food was probably fine, but she hadn't wanted to see anyone who might recognize her. She still didn't, but she'd take the chance if it meant Charlie wouldn't have to eat her cooking. "I don't particularly, but...Charlie, I'm a terrible cook. I'm trying to spare you the misery."

He stared at her for a long moment before he spoke. "Two things. I can't go into a nice restaurant looking like this." He pointed to his now grubby t-shirt.

She frowned as desperation gripped harder.

"Second, if you need someone to show you how to cook a grilled cheese, I'm your man."

Shivers raced over her at the thought of being alone in her kitchen with him. "But then you'd be cooking and not me."

"No. You cook. I'll supervise."

She studied his face for a long moment, looking for signs of the flirtatious guy who'd first hit on her. Nothing.

"Come on. We both win. I get dinner. You get a free cooking lesson."

There was no way she could refuse without hating herself. "Okay. But you've been warned."

He chuckled. "You don't scare me."

Maybe not. But he sure scared the hell out of her.

7

Laurel directed Charlie as he backed his truck until he was a few feet from the barn. She lifted her hand to indicate he should stop. Taillights flared, and then he cut the engine.

Her heart did a stupid little skip-jump thing as he emerged and strode toward her. *Careful,* her conscience reminded her. A man like him, magnetic in a reckless way, was nothing but trouble. There was a reason he could get any woman he wanted. Resisting those eyes, green as the grass she walked on, would be difficult for many women.

Dogs out in the fenced yard yipped and barked to acknowledge their presence. They probably wanted food, too, but she'd see to them soon. First, she needed to handle this load and the alluring guy who'd come along for the ride.

Laurel swallowed to settle the fluttering in her heart. "We can use the four-wheeler to transport them to the storage area in the back. Let me get it."

The feel of his eyes on her as she walked away burned. She tried to convince herself he wasn't looking and then had to glance back to know.

He shifted his gaze to the side as she turned.

He watched, but he didn't want her to know. Embers of attraction still smoldered. The knowledge excited her and scared her simultaneously. She didn't want a man like him, but knowing she could attract him did wonders for her ego.

In the corner of the barn, she lifted the trailer's hitch and hooked it to their four-wheeler.

"I can help with that," he called to her.

She was used to pulling her weight. "Got it."

A few seconds later, she drove the ATV toward him. Something sexy flickered in his gaze and fanned the flames singeing her senses. She glanced at the truck as he lowered the tailgate and refocused on the task at hand.

She'd allowed him to do all the heavy lifting earlier, but dragging bags down from the truck was much easier work. He hefted a bag and placed it on the trailer. As he did, she grabbed the corner of a bag and pulled it to the edge.

"Really, I can do this."

She eyed him with a look that warned him not to challenge her. "Really, so can I. How do you think I've managed all this time without you?"

His grin whipped through her heart and spun her senseless. "Rather poorly, I'd think."

Something warm and addictive blossomed in her heart. He'd returned to flirting. She should shut him down, but she'd missed it and savored the feeling for a moment. When she found the right man for her, she expected she'd experience something similar. "Is that so?"

He shrugged and hefted another bag onto the pile. "Nothing wrong with having a man around," he said under his breath.

She could argue, but it would be pointless since he was right on that account. She'd convinced herself she'd be fine if she lived alone for the rest of her life. But now that she'd experienced this kind of attention, attraction, and, let's face it, help, she wanted someone in her life.

The right someone, of course.

He hefted, and she dragged bags onto the trailer until they'd loaded it down. She then climbed down, straddled the four-wheeler, and maneuvered it until she'd backed it into the room where they stored food. Charlie had followed behind, and together they unloaded and stacked their haul. They repeated the process until they'd moved all the bags.

She wiped her sweaty brow as she strode toward the ATV once again. "That's a lot of dog food."

He tipped his head in agreement. "It's going to help a lot of dogs."

He looked as worn out as she felt, but she still couldn't resist a smile. "Yes, it will, and I'm grateful for each morsel."

"How many dogs are you housing right now?"

"Five. Two mutts, a boxer, another that looks like a golden lab mix, and then a cute little German Shepard puppy who's been hanging out in the house with me until he's bigger. I named him Jasper. He still needs puppy food, and I don't want the bigger dogs to eat it or trample him."

He kept his gaze focused on her while she spoke, as though each word interested him. She wished she could look away to slow the unnerving pulsing in her veins, but she couldn't.

"Three cats, too," she continued. "Also, a parrot. Jeanine, down at Anderson's store—you probably know her." She continued at his nod. "Her son begged for a bird, but it turns out his little sister is deathly allergic, so I said Geronimo could stay here until we find him a new home." *Why did he have to look at her that way?* "Are you interested? He comes with a cage and everything."

His eyes crinkled at the corners when he smiled. "Nah, I'm not much of a bird person."

She shrugged. "Me, either."

He eyed her with what looked like appreciation. "How do you manage to write on top of all this?"

"The animals? They're easy. Most of the time I prefer pets to people, and it's not like I write twenty-four seven."

His eyes narrowed with interest. "Why pets instead of people?"

"They are what they seem, so they're easier to trust." The instant she spoke, she regretted giving away so much personal information.

"I see."

Did he? She swore he could see right through her, but how could he really know her soul?

He lifted his chin. "Who watches them when you take a vacation?"

"Afton. Or Corey."

He nodded. "You can always call me, too. Unless you decide to invite me along. I'm always up for a new adventure."

"Adventure?" That word hit a little close to home.

He shrugged. "Aren't all vacations an adventure?"

She studied him for a long moment, trying to discern if his comments were genuine, or if something unseen lay beneath. "Thanks. But I usually go alone when I need to get away. I like the solitude and peace from being by myself."

He didn't seem offended by her response. "I understand. I like to run away at times, too."

She tilted her head, wishing she could stop the flow of conversation, but the man intrigued her. "If you could run away right now, where would you go?"

"With you or alone?"

Heat sizzled through her, and she worked to keep her composure. "Alone."

He narrowed his gaze as though thinking through several

possibilities. "The Netherlands, Ireland, and Spain all sound fantastic if I was traveling with someone. But I think I'd probably stick somewhere closer to home if I went by myself. You know, I've always thought it would be great to load a backpack and trek along the Pacific Northwest Trail. If I could get lost for a week and have nothing to do but soak up nature, that would be pretty damn cool."

She stared at him for a long moment.

"What?" he finally asked.

"I'd actually considered going there this fall."

He seemed surprised. "Seriously? Well, you know what they say about great minds. What would you do if you ran into a bear or another aggressive animal?"

She shrugged off his question. "I keep a gun with me whenever I'm anywhere that makes me vulnerable."

"Huh." He nodded in appreciation. "I didn't take you for the shooting type."

"Just goes to show you can't judge people by their appearance. My mom and I both learned when I was twelve. Girls need to know how to protect themselves."

He widened his eyes. "At twelve? Shouldn't a girl's parents be watching out for her instead?"

Her insides chilled as memories climbed to the surface. "Sometimes that's not always possible."

She needed to end their conversation. Now. She inhaled and released a deep breath. "I guess we should see about dinner."

He pulled a phone from his pocket. "It's only four. If you don't mind postponing for a bit, I could use a quick shower. I can check on Max while I'm there and let him outside for a few minutes."

She hated to wait even one more second. The longer Charlie hung around, the more chance he had to woo her, and the harder she had to fight her feelings.

But a cool shower to wash away the sweat and grime of their day, not to mention the effects of their most recent conversation, sounded heavenly. "Of course, that's fine. Be back in an hour? That will give me time to pull out stuff for those grilled cheeses we're making."

He grinned. "They're going to be the best damn grilled cheeses you've ever tasted."

She snorted. "You're forgetting, I'm one of the rare breeds who can screw up something that simple without even trying."

He cocked his brow. "*You're* forgetting that I'll be right there watching every step."

That was what worried her most.

He ran the tips of his fingers over the scruff on his chin as he studied her thoughtfully. "Do you have any chicken?"

She nodded.

"Garlic? Potatoes?"

"I have both."

"Perfect. How about I teach you a simple, easy meal that tastes like it took you a lot longer than it really does?"

The idea of learning to cook something tasty and easy appealed to her. "That actually sounds like fun."

A twinkle sparkled in his eyes. "It will be. Just wait and see."

Her heart tightened again, and she cursed it. Friendship was all she would offer this man, and her damned hormones needed to respect her decision.

The moment Charlie pulled away in his truck, she raced toward the house. She didn't have long to shower and get dressed before he returned.

8

Laurel left her hair damp to dry on its own and refused to put on more than a touch of makeup. She didn't want Charlie to think this was a date, or that she was trying to impress him. The man was a fireball, and she didn't need to add any fuel to an already potentially explosive situation. The night would go much smoother if she squelched any, and all, flirtations from the get-go.

She quickly fed the shelter animals and little Jasper before she hurried into the kitchen and gathered the ingredients he'd asked for. She removed the short, squatty candles from the table and set them on a nearby windowsill. No romance here.

The sound of an approaching vehicle halted any further preparations, and she hurried to open the front door for Charlie. When she found her mother on the other side of the door, her dark hair shot with silver pulled back and wearing lime green scrubs, she nearly died.

Her mom *could not* be there when Charlie showed up. She'd never hear the end of it. Her mother was already concerned a heartbreak might set her back emotionally. She wished she could say she wasn't as well.

In fact, she was certain the only reasons her mom let her go to college was that, first, she owned a gun, and second, she had absolutely zero interest in socializing.

She'd gone on wild adventures instead. Her mom had come unglued when she'd discovered the file of articles accounting Laurel's adventures, and they'd had a huge fight.

Still, she was grateful for that day. It wasn't until then that she realized how much Abercrombie had scarred her mother as well. She could only imagine the horror of finding out she'd left her precious daughter with a monster. From then on, she'd tried to forgive her mom for her overbearing behavior when she could.

"Hey, Mama. What are you doing here?"

Her mother lifted suspicious brows. "Since when do I need a reason to visit my daughter?"

Laurel swallowed as she worked to puzzle her way out of the pending disaster. "You don't, of course. I'm just surprised to see you. Usually, you call first to make sure I'm here."

Joanna shrugged and smiled. "I happened to be on my way home from town and thought I'd share my good news in person."

Please mom, make it quick. "Good news?" She did her best to seem appropriately interested lest she be called on the carpet for that, too.

"I found a date for you."

Her mother's words were a cool bucket of water poured straight over her head. *"You what?"*

"Since you're so insistent upon dating, I found someone mild-mannered and kind. A guy who's not likely to break your heart."

Why, oh why, did she ever mention dating to her mom? "Uh...thanks, Mama. But really, I'd like to find my own dates."

Joanna's gaze deepened with concern. "You need to be careful, Laurel."

She blinked a few times as she stared at her mom. "I'm a grown woman, capable of making good decisions."

Her mother waved away her response with an annoyed whisk of her hand. "Don't get your feathers all in a ruffle. It's only one date. I happened upon Riley LeMaye as he was coming out of the hardware store, and it just hit me. The guy is exactly who you described. Hard-working, loyal, a bit on the shy side. The guy's already taken over managing his dad's farm. I know his mama well and know she raised a good boy. Give him a chance."

Riley LeMaye? Not the best-looking guy around. But that might make him more likely to be sweeter, more attentive. Someone she could build a life with. Someone who'd always be there for her. She certainly wouldn't have to worry about him looking at other women. "I guess."

"Perfect. I gave him your number. He seemed interested."

She rolled her eyes. "Thanks, Mama." If they worked out as a couple, she'd never hear the end of that, either.

From the corner of her eye, she caught sight of Charlie's truck coming down the road and panic attacked her like an angry magpie. "I was just about to clean my bathroom, so..." She thumbed over her shoulder toward the house.

"Oh, doesn't that sound fun?" Joanna wrinkled her nose in distaste. "I should let you get to it, then."

She released a grateful breath. "Sounds good."

Her mom turned and then stopped. "I almost forgot to tell you. Your Aunt Georgia fell the other day and broke a hip. I only know because they brought her into the medical center."

"That's terrible." She had less than twenty seconds to get her mother in her car and on her way. She linked her arm around her mom's elbow and began walking toward her car.

"I wouldn't even care, except she was the only nice person

in your father's family. You should stop and see her."

Laurel opened the car door. "I don't even know her."

"Maybe it's time you did. I feel bad that you don't have any relatives that you see other than me."

"It's okay, Mama. I'm happy with who I have in my life." She contemplated shoving her mother into her car. "I'd better get to that bathroom."

"Oh. One more thing."

And that was that. Charlie slowed to turn into her drive, and her opportunity for a peaceful existence crashed down around her.

At the sound of his engine growing closer, Joanna cranked her head around. "Who's that?"

"A friend of Afton's. He adopted one of our dogs from the shelter."

She squinted as he parked next to her mom's car. "I don't think I know him. Does he live here in Aspen?"

"Yes, Mama. He's a partner in Afton's distillery."

"What's he doing here?" Joanna asked as he exited his truck.

As Charlie approached, Laurel glanced toward him with what she hoped was a friendly, but not too friendly look. "Hey, Charlie."

He looked good. Damn good. He'd changed into a button-down black shirt that emphasized the scruff on his chin and deepened his green eyes. The sight of him left her tingling everywhere, and she inhaled the scent of his woodsy, masculine cologne like she couldn't get enough air. He glanced between them and smiled, decimating her determined will. "Hey."

"I'd like to introduce you to my mama, Joanna Ewing. Mama, this is Charlie Blackmore. I was just telling Mama that you're here to pick up some of that dog food that was donated to the shelter."

His brows drew together in question but eased when he caught her frantic, conspiratorial look. "That's right. I sure appreciate it."

Laurel turned to her mom. "It's in the barn and I need to show him which bag, so I won't keep you."

Joanna glanced repeatedly between the two of them. "I could stay."

"No need." Laurel opened her car door farther. "Charlie will only be here a minute, and then I've got to clean the bathroom. No worries, Mama. Charlie's a friend of Afton's. She knows him well."

The code words they'd often used while Laurel was growing up, *someone knows him well*, seemed to work. Her mother gave Charlie a smile, though a heavy dose of uncertainty accompanied it, and she sank into her seat.

Laurel waited until her mom had started her car and put it into drive.

"Come with me," Laurel said in hushed tones, though there was no way her mother could hear, and she strode toward the barn. At the doorway, she stopped and glanced at the road. Her mother had stopped longer than necessary, but now she pulled out onto the street.

Laurel sagged her shoulders and sighed. "Sorry about that."

Charlie gave her a curious smile. "What was that all about?"

She turned toward the house and strode in that direction. "Don't ask," she called over her shoulder. A layer of guilt followed her along with an extremely attractive, but off-limits guy. She hated that she'd lied to her mom, but telling the truth would only upset her. If she was dating Charlie, she would have said so, but she wasn't, and she had no intention of doing so.

Case closed.

She jerked open the front door, stepped inside and held it

for Charlie, who'd stopped to grab a brown paper bag from his truck.

"Are you sure everything is okay?" he asked as he entered her house and she closed the door.

She exhaled a breath she hoped would cleanse the experience from her mind. "Yes. I'm great. My mama can be a pain in the ass, but whose isn't from time to time?"

"At least she cares. My mother lives in Vermont. I haven't heard from her since..." He lifted his gaze skyward. "Christmas."

"Ouch." She understood his pain. She'd never met her own father. "That's tough."

"It's not entirely her fault. My father can be a complete ass, and I'm sure she moved to the other side of the country to escape him. We were all older when they divorced, with our own lives, most of which revolved around my father's business, so she probably didn't have a chance."

"Still, it hurts."

He nodded solemnly. "Yeah."

She needed to get them off this downer track before she sank so low she wouldn't be able to pull herself out. "So, dinner?"

His serious look flipped into a grin. "Yes, dinner. I've been looking forward to this since you invited me. I brought fresh green beans and a bottle of Chardonnay. I hope you like them."

Her stomach grumbled at the thought of what could be a fantastic meal, if he didn't let her mess up. "Love them."

"Great. Let's get cracking. I'm starving." He stepped past her and headed toward the kitchen like he owned the place. He set down his offerings next to her pile of ingredients and frowned. "Oh."

The sound of disappointment in his voice raised panic inside her. "What's wrong?"

He laughed. "Nothing. Don't worry. When I asked about

chicken, I'd been thinking of a fresh, whole chicken, not frozen chicken breasts, and real garlic, not powdered. Fresh ingredients are best, but we can make this work."

She stepped forward, frustration nipping at her heels. "Sorry. I usually only cook for one, when I cook, so buying a whole chicken is pointless." Never in her life had she used fresh garlic, though she loved the flavor.

He shook his head. "Not with roasted chicken. You can use the leftovers in so many things."

She was certain incredulity lay heavy in her expression. "I really don't cook much."

He touched the tip of her nose with a forefinger. "Don't worry about it. This will be great." He gripped the wine bottle and strode toward her fridge, setting it inside.

She watched with uncertainty as he dominated her kitchen. He opened drawers and cabinets until he found a cutting board and her largest cutting knife. "I'll need a colander, a two-quart pot, a one-quart pot, and a small roasting pan."

She fetched the first three items with no problem and then paused. "By roasting pan, do you mean..." She let her sentence trail off, hoping he'd take the hint.

His brows rose toward his hairline, and he chuckled. But thankfully, he kept any derisive comments to himself. "Shallow pan, a few inches deep. A casserole dish will work."

Relief flooded her. "Of course. I knew that." Or at least she should have.

She set the pan on the counter and glanced at their ever-growing pile of dishes and ingredients.

For a good half-hour, she melted butter and salt to pour over the chicken breasts before baking, peeled potatoes, and washed green beans. Flirtation ceased to exist as he instructed her on each detail. He apparently took cooking seriously, and she appreciated that.

Twenty minutes before dinner was served, he pulled the wine from the fridge and helped her start cooking the beans. He instructed her on the fine art of mashing potatoes while he removed her colorful china from a cabinet.

"Drop a good half a cube of butter in there. While it's melting, add a half a cup of milk. Cream is better if you have it, and a quarter teaspoon of garlic." He held up a burgundy and a slate green plate, interrupting her train of thought. "I like these colors together. Nice."

She smiled, glad he approved of at least one thing in her kitchen. "Thank you."

She whipped potatoes with her small hand-held mixer like a pro as the beans boiled. When it was time, he bumped her with his hip, indicating she needed to step aside while he pulled the chicken from the oven. His friendliness seemed natural and right, and she was grateful for it.

Heavenly scents of garlic and a beautifully browned chicken filled the room. *She was doing this*, creating a home-cooked meal, and the whole domesticated silliness made her happy.

She ejected the small beaters from her mixer and tapped them on the edge of the pan. "My mom worked a lot of evening and night shifts when I was younger. When she was home, she was usually exhausted, so we ate a lot of simple stuff, frozen stuff, or just plain cereal."

He studied her with a sideways glance. "What does your mom do for a living?"

"She's a nurse. At the medical center in Pinecone."

He poured wine into their glasses. "Just you and your mom?"

"Yep. The two musketeers, as she likes to say." As hard as life had been at times, she loved her mom with all her heart and admired her greatly. They'd both had their challenges, and her mom had remained strong through it all.

"So you what, stayed with grandma while your mom worked nights when you were little?"

Her stomach clenched. *Leave the past in the past. It's not your future.* "With a neighbor until I was older, until we moved to Aspen."

"You originally lived in Pinecone?"

Her counselor could give her all the mantras she wanted. They helped. Sometimes. But she'd realized she needed to keep her from going to that darkness in the first place. Pushed to the edge, she laughed to break the conversation. "Are you going to keep grilling me, or are we going to eat? I'm starving."

He lifted one corner of his mouth into an engaging smile. "Just trying to get to know you better."

She scooped the potatoes into a large serving bowl. They'd made far too much, which meant only one thing. *Leftovers,* something good to look forward to. Those were the things that kept her in a forward motion. "I think it's my turn to grill you, then. Where did *you* grow up?"

He placed the chicken breasts on a platter and carried them to the table. "Salt Lake."

She returned for the beans. "From Salt Lake to Aspen. That's quite a change."

"I like it. Small town life suits me." He waited by a chair but didn't sit, and she realized he held it for her.

Her gaze met his as she approached and scary, delicious sensations danced inside her. *Dammit.* She settled into her chair, and he took the seat next to her instead of across the table. She swallowed, trying to dispel the butterfly wings beating inside her as she and Charlie filled their plates. "Don't you miss your family?"

He barked a laugh. "Hardly."

Then held up a hand. "I take that back. I miss my mom sometimes. But my dad and cutthroat corporate brothers? Nah.

We're too different. They can have their crazy, stress-filled worlds. I'll live here."

"And cook," she added. "An admirable profession."

He grinned. "Not without its stress, either, but it's a good kind of stress. One that will lessen once we've opened the restaurant."

"Afton says the test grand opening will be her wedding reception."

Teasing glinted in his eyes. "Brave of her, don't you think? What if I totally blow it?"

"You won't." She laid her napkin across her lap, giving her an excuse to look away from his mesmerizing eyes. "You said you've cooked for Afton and Corey before, so I'm sure they know what they're in for. Also, Afton mentioned it was a good way to showcase your talents. I think it's brilliant."

He tilted his head and looked at her a little more closely. "Brilliant? Huh. I'm not sure I've ever been called brilliant."

Heat rushed up her cheeks. She hadn't meant to be so bold with her flattery. "Then maybe just very smart."

He lifted his wine glass as though toasting her. "I'll take brilliant."

To break the intensity sparking between them, she lifted her fork and knife, cut into the chicken, and slid the bite into her mouth.

"Oh, my gosh." She lifted her fingers to cover her mouthful of food. "This is incredible. I can't believe it tastes so good with only those few ingredients."

He shrugged, but she could tell he basked in her compliment. "Told you. Cooking isn't that difficult. You might find you even like it."

She nodded, thinking he might be right. Nothing like a success to make her want to try again. "I'm going to invite my mom over for dinner and serve this. She'll be beyond shocked."

"I'll give you a recipe for an easy cheesecake. Then she'll really be impressed."

He lifted a forkful of potatoes into his mouth. A second later, he widened his eyes, and then visibly swallowed the potatoes with a pained expression coloring his features. Horror filled her.

He choked as he lifted his wine and then took a long drink. "How much garlic did you put in these?"

The happy moment they'd created crumbled like dry toast. Her thoughts raced as she tried to remember what she'd done, while she also searched for a way to salvage their dinner. Both only succeeded in a deep sense of self-disappointment and overwhelming humiliation. "Just what you said. A teaspoon."

A laugh erupted from him that deepened her embarrassment. "A teaspoon? I said a quarter of a teaspoon."

She shook her head, trying to remember clearly. "Oh, God. I never should have attempted..." Her throat closed over the rest of her words.

"No, no, no. Shit." He shifted in his chair until his knees touched the side of her thigh, and he took her hand, folding it between his.

"Please don't feel bad. I'm sorry I laughed, Laurel. You caught me by surprise. This is my fault. I should have watched you closer."

She tucked her lips inward and shook her head. She wanted to speak, but she was afraid her words would fail, and she'd make a bigger fool of herself.

He gave her a gentle smile and tugged on her hand, pulling her closer to him. When she was close enough, he enveloped her with a hug, forcing her face close to his warm neck. She froze, shocked by the sensations rolling through her.

"The one thing about learning to be a chef is that eventually you're going to screw something up. We call it a discovery instead of a mistake." His voice rumbled in her ear, soothing her. "Trust me. I've discovered a shit-ton of things the hard way. The worst was when I'd cooked for my whole family right after I'd announced that I quit the family business so that I could attend culinary school. I planned this crazy, impressive menu for that night for dinner, and I flopped."

"You did?" She sniffed as she pulled back so she could see his face. "What did they say?"

Pain flickered in his eyes and tugged on her heart. "My father left the table, offering to buy a proper dinner for anyone who wanted to go."

She ached for what must have been an enormous disappointment for him. "Did anyone leave?"

"My brothers both did. I'm sure they all had a great laugh at my expense."

His father sounded like a huge jerk. "That's terrible."

"Like I said, it's all part of being a chef. I salvaged the beef wellington somewhat, and I whipped up some quick potatoes like these."

She tried to pout but couldn't. "Not exactly like these."

He smiled. "No, not exactly. The cherries jubilee I made for dessert was excellent, but no one stuck around for it. All in all, I wasn't a complete failure. Just like you're not, either. The chicken is perfect, and I couldn't have done better with the green beans."

"You're just saying that to make me feel better."

"Taste for yourself." He squeezed her hand and then released her. "Don't let one little thing ruin this night for us, Laurel."

This night...for us? His words implied it held some significance for him, but how much? And could she be okay with that? "Thanks for sharing your story with me. It helps."

"Good. Let's eat the rest of this before it gets cold."

9

Laurel lingered at the table with Charlie long after they'd finished their meal, long past when she should have told him goodnight. She couldn't deny she enjoyed his company. But friends often did the same.

The fact that her insides tightened every time he looked directly into her eyes would have no bearing on their relationship. He was an attractive man. She could admit that, too. Didn't mean she'd act on it.

She knew what she wanted out of life, and he wasn't it.

"I should probably get to those dishes," she finally said, not wanting to end their evening, but knowing it was time. "I still have an article I need to work on tonight, and it's almost nine."

He glanced at the clock on the wall and seemed as surprised as she was that it was so late. "Let's get those dishes done, and then I'll go."

"No, you go. I'll let them soak while I work, and then they'll be a breeze."

"That's not fair to make you cook *and* clean."

Her thoughts faded to a scene with them both standing side

by side at the sink. Dishes seemed so much more fun with him in the picture.

Which was a problem. She needed to end the evening before her thoughts strayed to something more romantic once again. "Really. It's fine. There aren't many."

They stood at the same time, and she found herself only inches from him. The low buzz that had been humming in her veins all night jumped to something akin to an electric shock, and she lifted her gaze to his face. He was so tall. So handsome.

So close.

She swallowed and took a step back, needing distance. "Thanks again for helping me today. The doggies thank you, too." As casually as she could, she led the way to the front door.

"No problem." His voice came from close behind her. "I admire what you ladies are doing, and I'm happy to help whenever you need it."

She opened the front door before she turned to look at him.

Again, so close. The look he gave her made it hard to breathe.

He hesitated and then stepped outside. "Call me whenever you want, okay?"

"Okay." Her voice came out far more breathless than she wanted.

He hesitated for a long moment, each second causing an increase in her pulse. All thoughts of this-was-not-a-date skittered away, and she wondered if he'd try to kiss her. *What would she do if he did?*

She scrambled to think of something to break the moment, but all she could imagine was what it would be like to have those lips on hers. Just a little taste.

His gaze bored deep into hers. Her heartbeats grew excruciatingly intense. Then he blinked. "Have a good night, Laurel."

Wait. *What?*

He turned and stepped off her porch, his stride quick and sure as he made his way to his truck. She grabbed the doorframe and watched. This man messed with her head far more than she should let him.

"You, too," she called to his retreating form.

Lost over what to do next, she stayed put until he started his engine. Then she forced herself back inside the house and closed the door on what was a memorable but unsettling evening. She dropped into a nearby chair and immediately replayed the events in her mind.

She'd been sure they were only friends.

Then not. Then friends. Then... How could she know the difference? Her experience was extremely limited. No one, except her mom, including Afton, knew that she'd never kissed a boy, let alone a man.

She should have done it back in fifth grade when her friends had dared her to kiss the boy she'd liked in school. She could have gotten it out of the way before her life shattered. Maybe then she wouldn't be so susceptible to Charlie and his charms.

A knock on the door startled her, and she jumped to her feet. Charlie must have forgotten something.

She opened the door with an expectant look. Without hesitating, he slipped an arm around her waist and pulled her hard against him. Stunned and out of her mind with excitement, she didn't resist. He slid a hand around the back of her neck and held her as he lowered his mouth to hers.

Exquisite sensations exploded the second his lips touched hers. His expert kisses drew her into a tangled web where she needed nothing but him. Her traitorous body molded to his, and delicious pleasure radiated from each place they touched.

When he teased her lips with his tongue, she opened instinctively, hungry for more of what he offered. She'd never experienced anything so sensual, and her starved body and mind craved more.

Without warning, he broke the kiss. His look remained intent, without a hint of a smile. "There. That ought to do it."

He turned, strode back to his truck, and started the engine. He caught her gaze for a second before he pulled away.

She could only stare. She had nothing to compare to Charlie's kiss, but she knew her first kiss was nothing short of epic.

His taillights disappeared into the distance, leaving an unwelcome ache deep in her heart.

"No," she whispered as the cool evening air encompassed her. That never was supposed to happen. Worse, she couldn't regret that it had.

10

Laurel added a new pair of crystal earrings her mother had given her to commemorate her date with Riley. That her mom had set this up was a tremendous shift in attitude about her daughter dating. But that her mom had picked her date still bothered her. They'd be discussing the issue soon.

For tonight, she would let it all go and pretend she was normal. The earrings went well with the sheer lavender shirt she wore over a white cami. As she studied herself in the mirror, a smile slowly curved her lips. As hard as life could be, the person she'd been two years ago when she'd reentered therapy wouldn't recognize the woman of today, and she was grateful for that.

In the past, she'd always dressed for comfort and anonymity instead of flash. After she'd moved to Aspen with her mom, her classmates had questioned why she wanted to be so plain. She couldn't explain. They wouldn't understand. They would have said she should be glad Abercrombie hadn't hurt her like he had the other girls, and that, yes, it was a crazy ordeal, but that shouldn't make her so afraid of men. The one evil man who'd touched her life was behind bars for a lifetime.

They'd say nothing had happened to *her*. Like the residents in Pinecone had. She was alive and unharmed. Sure, they had pity for her, but not like they did for the families of the other victims. Even for her, each time she saw someone from those families, guilt and shame burned her. *She'd lived.* Their children hadn't.

Her scars might not be physical, they might not be logical, but they were very real to her. And she was afraid.

At least she had been. She'd worked hard for a very long time to overcome those fears. She'd finally found a place where she could consider her future, but that didn't mean past fears weren't still there. She'd wrangled them into submission, but they hovered beneath the surface, waiting to poke and prod her every time she dared to step forward.

Yet, here she was. Dressed to impress, looking flirty and maybe a little sexy, if she dared say so herself. Even if she was terrified on the inside, she'd come this far. She could go farther.

Who knew? This date could be the one. Riley was a few years older than her, and she'd never interacted with him at social functions. But from what she'd heard, he was about as strong, solid, and steady as they came. Maybe he would like her, too. Maybe this could develop into something rich and romantic, and they could spend their lives living happily together.

Maybe this relationship would finally set her free from the past.

Her stomach filled with nervous flutterings again, reminding her of her first date with Charlie. That hadn't worked out so well. But this one might. She had to hold on to that.

She spritzed on perfume, glossed her lips, and then released a large breath full of pent-up nerves and energy. This was all a necessary part of dating. Average was what she strived for, just like her counselor had advised. Anything more, and she would set herself up for failure. Everyone wanted the perfect man. She would be happy with a good one.

The doorbell rang and startled her out of her reverie. She stood, working to get her head back in the game. *This was good*. Whether her date was a flop, she could say she'd joined the dating game, something very common for women her age. She wanted a normal life, and that's exactly what she was claiming. If nothing else, she was proud of herself for that.

Jasper barked at her heels as she opened the front door.

Her first impression of Riley was that he reminded her of a washed-out watercolor painting. Although he was tall, his sandy blonde hair and pale blue eyes seemed to lack depth. Still, he had a friendly smile, and that counted for something. Looks were not everything, and they faded fast. Perhaps once she knew him well enough, she could fall in love with the person inside.

She smiled to welcome him. "Hi Riley."

"Hello Laurel."

A few endless seconds stretched between them, urging her to say or do something to break the ice. "I suppose in a town this small, it's time we finally met." Pushing herself out of her comfort zone, she leaned forward and gave him a quick hug, like Afton always did with her friends.

He stiffened, and she immediately pulled away, wondering if she'd broken some kind of first date code. Uncomfortable awkwardness filtered through her as she stepped back and looked away from his pale face.

She lifted Jasper from the floor, her heart growing warm as it did every time she looked into those deep brown eyes. "Let me put my dog in his kennel, and I'll be ready to go."

Riley watched as Jasper's pink tongue lolled out the side of his mouth as if it was too much work to keep inside. Laurel laughed and expected Riley to ruffle his soft fur or comment on how cute he was. He said nothing. Her happiness cooled as she walked toward a back bedroom, where she deposited Jasper into his puppy crate.

"Do you have pets?" she asked when she returned.

"Three horses."

He opened the front door for her, and she stepped outside, chuckling inwardly at his silliness. "I mean cats, dogs, birds. Anything you keep specifically as a pet."

He gave a brief shake of his head before he opened the passenger door of his very new, very nice black truck. "I have some allergy concerns."

Concerns? What exactly did that mean?

She let the question slide without further probing as Riley claimed the driver's seat, started the engine, and headed toward the highway. It wasn't as if she couldn't be with someone who was allergic to animals.

Granted, it would be awfully hard to imagine life without a sweet puppy or kitty in her house. But she always had the shelter, and those pets needed lots of love and attention. If he was truly the right guy for her, his allergies wouldn't be a dealbreaker. It wasn't like he could help what he was allergic to.

With that thought, she released her worries. Just like she had when Riley had contacted her about their date. He didn't say where they were going, and she didn't ask. He'd only mentioned the day and time. She'd go with the flow instead of worry. She'd stressed too much about dinner with Charlie, and she promised her counselor she would relinquish control and have faith that things would work out okay. Not always easy for her, but she was taking life in a new direction now.

Luckily, Riley had decided Sparrow's was a good option

instead of traipsing into Pinecone. She would have gone along with whatever, but this way was much less stressful.

Riley held his body ramrod straight as they entered the bar and grill, and his awkwardness spilled over onto her. He was probably as nervous as she was, and she needed to give him a break.

He held her chair for her as they claimed a table near the door, and she silently appreciated his gentlemanly gesture. Still, she needed to break the ice, or her anxiety would hit the roof. "Have you ever tried the chicken pot pie here?"

He sat across from her and picked up a menu. "Yeah."

She stared at him for a long moment while he perused it. *Yeah?* Was that the extent of his answer? "How about the chili and cornbread?"

He spared her a brief glance then, his features diminished by the darkened interior. "I've lived in Aspen my whole life, which has given me a lot of time to try everything on the menu."

"Okay." She laughed, although he'd once again shot down her track of conversation without replacing it with anything else.

The server came to take their orders, giving her a sly glance, hinting that she recognized Laurel was with a different man than she had been a few weeks ago. Laurel ignored her.

As Becky walked away, Laurel remained quiet, determined Riley would rekindle the conversation this time. He glanced about the room instead, seeming happy to sit in silence. Seriously though, what was the point of dating if she wasn't going to get to know the man better? Her mom had said he was shy, but there was a difference between shyness and acting like a zombie.

Apparently, she'd have to be the one to carry the conversation. "My mom said you're taking over your father's farm. That sounds interesting."

His eyes lit up. "I cut two fields of alfalfa this morning. Raccoons got into the barn last night and made a mess, so that took me a while to clean up. Damn varmints."

She'd encountered a few raccoons in the wild but had never gotten super close. "I've heard raccoons can be mean. Were they still there this morning?"

"No."

Although she'd grown up in small farming communities, she didn't know much about the day-to-day activities of a farmer, and she struggled to find something to talk about. "Do you have someone who helps you?"

"Just my dad. When he's up to it."

She spent the next fifteen minutes searching for something to say. She'd ask a question, and he'd give her a short answer, leaving her struggling for the next thing to keep the conversation going.

She nearly gasped aloud in relief when their blond, buxom server brought their food. Riley didn't give Becky a second glance, which earned him one point in his favor. Unfortunately, he sadly lacked in other areas.

They ate in silence. Laurel pretended to enjoy the music blaring over the sound system and smiled at Riley whenever their gazes met.

Was she doing something wrong? She was a complete novice at dating, but she'd been around plenty of people. She'd never struggled to maintain a conversation like she did now. Was she not friendly enough? Not flirty enough to keep his attention?

She never struggled like this when she'd been with Charlie.

Just as she thought about him, Charlie walked in with Jerry Tierno, and she cringed. *Oh...damn.*

The dark-haired, handsome men both stole her attention, and she found it difficult to look away. Thankfully, they hadn't noticed her, but Sparrow's wasn't a big place. She glanced at Riley and realized he'd never save her from the awkwardness when Charlie did, so she focused on her mostly empty plate.

The embarrassment of having Charlie see her on her silent, awkward date wormed its way inside. She needed to appear to be having the time of her life in order to discourage him. She needed Charlie to know his kiss, the one that had scorched her dreams for weeks, meant nothing.

She brightened her smile and focused on Riley. "What do you do for fun?"

He grunted and shrugged. "By the time I get done in the fields, there's not a lot of time left for fun."

"You must do something," she prodded. She could not let this conversation die. "How about hiking? Or biking? Ever gone skydiving?"

He appeared to consider her question before he shook his head. "I usually have a beer and watch TV. Nothing wrong with kicking back and enjoying a cold one after a long day."

She nodded, encouraged by his lengthy reply, if not by the quality of his answer. "I'm sure farming takes a lot out of you. Do you ever have a chance to get away on the weekends, do anything for fun, then?"

"Not very often. I used to ride horses in the hills and sometimes camp, but I haven't done much of that lately."

Her nerves tightened when she spotted Charlie in her peripheral vision moving in their direction. She wouldn't look. *She would not look.* She was far too engrossed in her current date to give him the least amount of thought. "That sounds like fun." She bit her bottom lip, praying Charlie would move past their table without stopping.

"Yeah, but I've got responsibilities now. It takes too much time."

She felt him then, standing near her. Even so, she wouldn't look. "Everyone needs to make time for fun. You'll get old fast otherwise."

"She's right, Riley." Charlie stepped into her direct view now and held out his hand to Riley, who shook it even as Charlie's gaze slid to her. "Better listen to her."

Her heartbeat quickened at the sight of Charlie, looking dark and dangerous in black jeans and a tight gray t-shirt. She glanced between the two men, surprised at the difference in energy bouncing off them.

Riley offered a chilled smile and leaned back in his chair. "You ever run a farm, Blackmore?"

Charlie stared at him for a second longer than was comfortable for her. "Can't say that I have."

"Then you don't know what you're talking about, and you'd best leave us to our date."

Whoa. Apparently the mild-mannered, bland Riley had a dick side after all.

Charlie smirked. "Just trying to be friendly, LeMaye."

"You're an outsider, Blackmore. Stop pretending you belong."

Laurel's insides clenched. She never would have guessed Riley to be so rude. "I'm an outsider, too, Riley. I used to live in Pinecone."

He didn't take his gaze from Charlie. "That's different. Pinecone might as well be Aspen."

Charlie slid his gaze to her then, his eyes full of snarky disbelief. "Enjoy your evening."

With that, he strode away and joined Jerry at his table.

"Asshole," Riley whispered.

Laurel wiped her mouth with her napkin, set it on her plate, and pushed it away, signaling that she was done. Done with dinner, done with Riley, and most certainly done with dating. Testosterone did nothing but mess up her life.

"Are you finished?" Riley asked.

She had never been more finished in her life. "Quite."

11

Anger roiled inside Charlie as he strode to the table Jerry had claimed near the windows and dropped into a chair. *What the hell was that all about? Riley LeMaye? Seriously?* "Asshole."

Jerry raised his brows. "Who?"

He held his tongue for several long moments, knowing if he spoke sooner, he'd release a string of words that would make a trucker blush. "Laurel," he finally ground between his teeth.

Jerry flicked a glance in her general direction. "Laurel Ewing?"

He jerked his head in a nod.

Confusion furrowed Jerry's brows. "Did she say something to piss you off?"

"No. But if I could have ripped off Riley's head and shoved it up his ass, I'd feel a hell of a lot better."

Jerry held up a hand. "Wait a minute. Are you pissed at Laurel or at Riley?"

Hell if he knew. He was just pissed. He shook his head as Becky set two bottles of beer in front of them.

"I'm pissed at them both," he said, after waiting for Becky to walk away. The last thing he needed was for Laurel to hear her date had affected him. "Why the hell would Laurel lower herself to date such a cocky son-of-a-bitch? Riley's an asshole to the extreme. Why would she choose to be with a guy like that?"

Jerry shrugged, still seeming lost. "Because she likes him?"

Charlie narrowed a laser-sharp look and shot it at his friend. "Like I couldn't figure that much."

His friend laughed. "Dude. You keep this up, and I'm going to call you a jealous bitch. I didn't know you had the hots for Laurel."

He slugged down a fair amount of beer, wishing it would smother the fire in his heart. "*Had* is the keyword there."

"Over it already?" Jerry smirked. "Good luck with that."

He turned his irritation on his friend. "What the hell is that supposed to mean?"

"It means I know that look on your face. Saw it in the mirror every day when I was doing my best to hate Kimber after she dumped me. But the heart wants what the heart wants. You look like you want her pretty damn bad."

"Shit," he hissed under his breath. "I don't want anyone who doesn't want me."

Jerry snorted. "I know I don't get out as much now that I'm married, but when the hell were you dating Laurel? Or are you just pining after her, and she doesn't give a shit about you?"

"We dated. Twice. I brought her here, and then I gave her a cooking lesson at her house." His thoughts immediately jumped to their scorching kiss. He hadn't imagined the chemistry. There was no way he could have.

"Twice doesn't make her yours."

"No shit." He shook his head, trying to make sense of her actions. "But there was something between us, Jerry. I didn't imagine it."

Jerry leaned back in his chair and regarded him with a questioning gaze. "Are you sure?"

Charlie shot him a look that threatened to take off his head if he continued with his asinine questioning.

"If you're certain she liked you as well—"

"A woman doesn't kiss me like she did if she's not feeling it."

A sly grin crossed Jerry's face. "Well, if you think she liked you, too, and you didn't do anything to piss her off, then I'd say she's scared. As long as I've known her, she's always been a quiet, skittish kind of person. Only has a few good friends in town."

Jerry's rational thinking deflated Charlie's anger like a tiny hole in a balloon. "You think?" He couldn't help remember Corey's statement that Laurel didn't think he was her type, but that was before their kiss. So maybe fear was a factor.

Jerry twisted his bottle in a circle. "Maybe you need to give the lady some space."

No. "I gave her some space, and now she's with another guy."

He seemed to ponder that and then shrugged. "If it makes you feel better, she looked as miserable as you do right now."

Charlie straightened in his seat, appreciating that Jerry had the perfect vantage point to watch her on her date. "Really?"

"She's not happy. I can tell you that. LeMaye tried to hold her elbow as they left, but she jerked away."

He swiveled in his seat. "They're gone?" Son of a bitch. Now he'd have to wonder where they'd go and what they'd do next. He didn't want that asshole alone with her.

Jerry held up a hand. "Look, dude. Even if she had a good time on her date with Riley, they're not engaged. She's a single lady and fair game. You just need to figure out a good strategy to invade and conquer her heart."

He nodded. *Yes.* This was something he could grab onto. He might have lost the night's battle, but he was far from losing the war. His gut told him Laurel was a woman worth fighting for, and that's exactly what he intended to do.

He'd back off a little, like Jerry suggested. Let her know he wasn't a threat. He'd also find a way to be alone with her again, and when he did, he'd use everything in his arsenal to tempt her. He'd make her want him as much as he did her, and he'd also make sure she was the one who kissed him first the next time.

———

Laurel said very little to Riley on the way to her house, and he stayed quiet as well. Perhaps the entire experience had been less than satisfying for him, too. He didn't seem to mind the fact that they hadn't lingered at the restaurant like she had with Charlie. Their conversation had been engaging, but tonight, she couldn't get home fast enough.

The moment Riley pulled into her drive and shifted the truck into park, she opened her door and climbed out. She wanted as much distance between them as possible. He caught up with her quickly as she headed toward her porch, and he placed his hand on the doorknob as though he intended to maintain his status as a gentleman.

When he didn't open it right away, Laurel tilted her gaze upward. An unsettling half-smile lingered on Riley's lips, and he studied her with a look that made it obvious that he didn't find her as distasteful as she did him.

"I hope you had fun tonight," he said.

Though she'd like to speak the words tumbling through her mind, she couldn't be cruel like he was. The man bought her a meal, after all. She could show some appreciation. "My chicken was delicious. Thank you."

His smile widened. "That makes me happy."

Suddenly, they were back to the awkward man who'd first arrived at her door. The enraged beast who'd come out when Charlie was around had gone back into its cave once again. Even so, she was glad he'd taken her straight home after dinner.

He stared at her for a long moment, his expression growing quizzical. "What's that on your cheek?" He leaned close to inspect. Before she realized his intent, his mouth covered hers.

She jerked back in reaction. Her heart thundered as she fought the fight-or-flight instincts flooding her.

Riley smiled, oblivious to the look of disgust that was surely in her expression.

"Have a good night, Laurel." He walked away, whistling as he did.

Oh, good God. What the hell was wrong with that man?

And why did guys think they could kiss without asking?

If he hadn't walked away right then, she would have slapped him. Or at least given him a verbal lashing.

She shook off irritation and anger as she stepped inside her house and slammed the door. "Arrogant asshole," she hissed. He certainly wasn't the shy man she and her mom had both assumed. He wasn't an endearing quiet man, either. He was as boring as dirt unless he was being a jerk.

"Gah," she yelled. If she'd had any ridiculous thoughts of seeing him again, he'd blasted them to smithereens. She dragged the back of her hand across her lips, trying to wipe away any trace of him, but it did little to dispel the emotions churning inside her. He had no right to force himself on her. No right to—

A sudden rush of horrific memories tackled her, crushing

her lungs. Tortured nightmares generated by her younger self flooded in. Abercrombie, the neighbor who'd always had a smile for her, turned dark, his teeth rotting before her. He laughed as he held a faceless girl to the ground and—

"*No!*" Her voice echoed throughout the quiet house.

That was years and years ago.

Those girls were not being tortured right now.

Abercrombie was behind prison bars. Always would be.

She was fine. This was fine. She repeated the mantra until her breathing slowed.

Riley had kissed her. That was all. He did it through naivety. Not with an intent to harm.

There was no danger.

No fire.

She practiced calming breaths and turned her thoughts to cute little Jasper. Sweet puppy. Soft kisses. Loving snuggles.

She inhaled a deep breath and let it slide out as she made her way to Jasper's crate. He yipped and danced until she opened the door. Emotionally exhausted, she sank to the floor and let him love her with lots of licks and a few excited nips.

The darkness faded, and she breathed easier.

A small part of her offered congratulations for gaining self-control over the situation in such a short time. Years ago, things like this had sent her into hiding for days. She may not have completely conquered her reaction, but she'd done well.

A disturbing thought shoved its way to the surface. *Why hadn't Charlie's kiss done the same?* He'd also done so without asking.

The answer came hot on its tail.

The difference was she'd wanted Charlie's kiss. Wanted his lips on hers. Wanted to press up against him.

Worse, Charlie made her feel safe. Riley hadn't.

Charlie might make her heart pound as if she was on a roller coaster, but she'd enjoyed every minute she'd spent with him.

The discovery nearly undid her again. She gathered Jasper into her arms and hugged him. "Forget the rest of them. You're the only man I need in my life."

12

Laurel whipped potatoes, keeping one eye on the clock in her mom's kitchen as she did. Her mother should arrive in less than five minutes. When she spotted the familiar red Escort pulling into the drive, she shut off the mixer. Grabbing two oven mitts, Laurel pulled the roasted chicken from the oven just as Joanna walked into the house.

"Oh, my God. What smells so good?" Joanna glanced around her kitchen, her eyes growing wider as she took in the mess Laurel had left on the counter.

"I cooked," she said proudly.

Wonder sparkled in her mom's eyes. "I can see that."

Her own anticipation rose in accordance with her mom's reaction. "Wait until you taste it." She'd followed Charlie's instructions carefully, and this time, her potatoes rocked. She'd taste-tested a moment ago, just to be sure.

Joanna shrugged out of her pink nurse's scrub jacket. "Let me put down my things and wash. I'll be right back."

Laurel quickly set the table and had everything ready by the time her mom returned.

Joanna took her usual seat at the table. "What's the occasion?"

"Let's call it your last supper."

Her mom laughed. "My last supper?"

Laurel tossed her a smile full of pretend malice. "Before I murder you."

Joanna glanced at the dishes full of aromatic food. "If you've poisoned this beautiful meal, I'm going to be really mad."

It was Laurel's turn to laugh. She'd honestly been ticked at her mom for setting her up with Riley, but she could never stay mad for long. "I guess you'll have to trust me," she teased.

Joanna sliced off layers of chicken for each of them. Laurel slapped a pile of garlic mashed potatoes on her plate before she handed the bowl to her mother.

They dished up green beans and then her mom reached for the bottle of Chardonnay. "When did you learn how to cook?"

Sweet memories of her time with Charlie crept in and warmed her cheeks. "A friend taught me, though I'm not sure if learning to make one meal qualifies as learning to cook."

Joanna's gaze intensified. "A friend? Someone I know?"

"No." *Hell.* She couldn't lie again. "Actually, I believe you met him once, Mama. At my house. The guy who came to pick up dog food. Charlie?" She braced herself for her mom's reaction.

"Is that so?" Her mom wouldn't meet her gaze. "I'd wondered if there was something between the two of you."

"He's just a friend, Mama. Don't blow it out of proportion."

Her mom huffed. "Well, he didn't look at you like a friend."

He hadn't? "Doesn't matter. We're just friends." How did this conversation get focused on Charlie? She'd meant to show off her new cooking skills and impress her mom whilst also letting her know she needed to butt out of her love life, not this interrogation.

"If you say so."

"I do." She shot her a pointed look for emphasis. "I'm not dating Charlie, and if you ever try to set me up with Riley again, I *will* murder you."

Her mom looked up in surprise. "Why? Riley said you both had a fantastic time."

Laurel choked on the potatoes in her mouth and needed a sip of wine to clear them away before she could speak. "He did not."

"He did. Said you'd enjoyed dinner and had a lovely evening."

Her previous anger over Riley's behavior jumped to life like a rotting zombie. "If by a lovely evening, you mean he behaved like an ass in public, embarrassing me in front of one of my friends. *And then* he had the nerve to force an unwanted, disgusting kiss on me before he left. Then yes, we had a damn fine evening." She inhaled a deep breath after her long tirade.

The color drained from her mother's face as the atmosphere in the room chilled. "He forced a kiss on you?" she asked in a near whisper.

Laurel held her mother's gaze as she nodded. Her mom had been through every one of the ups and downs that had followed Abercrombie's arrest, and they'd both suffered.

"Are you okay?" her mom asked quietly.

She blinked a few times, ensuring her emotions were in check. "I am now. It messed with me a bit. But, you know what? I'm a stronger person these days."

A sad look crossed her mom's face, and she shook her head. "Oh, Laurel. I'm so sorry. If I would have had any clue..."

She snorted in derision. "We never do, do we? Someone we think of as perfectly fine turns out to be a monster. Not meaning Riley. He's just a clueless idiot."

"Who forced himself on a woman?" Her mother wasn't inclined to be as forgiving.

But with time came clarity. "Honestly, especially now that you've told me Riley's opinion of the evening, I believe he really thought I liked him."

"Being an idiot doesn't excuse his behavior. He'd better hope he doesn't run into me again anytime soon."

The last thing she needed was more drama. "Mama, please. Just let it go. I wanted to let you know what happened so you don't keep encouraging him, but please, let's just let it go. I can't hang on to this, okay?"

Joanna held her gaze for a long moment. "Okay, honey. Gone and forgotten. I promise to do my best to hold my tongue when I see him again."

Laurel relaxed and grinned. Like either of them believed her mom could keep her mouth shut if she had something to say. At least for now, she hopefully would temper her words.

Her mom sliced off another piece of chicken. "This is really very good, you know. Did it take you hours?"

She shook her head, grateful the topic of Riley was in the past. "It's pretty simple. Doesn't take long at all. Fresh ingredients are the secret to great flavor."

Joanna arched a dark brow. "Something *your friend* taught you?"

"Actually, yes."

Her mom stared at her while she chewed. "Charlie?"

"Yes, Charlie. He's a friend of Afton's, remember? He's opening the new restaurant at Sagecreek."

"Yes. I saw Afton at Rumors a few weeks ago, and she mentioned it, too."

She was heartened that her mom seemed interested. "It's something Charlie has wanted to do forever. I guess he broke some ties with his family when he pursued his dream. I admire that, you know. Someone willing to take a chance on something he really wants."

"Like you dating despite your history."

She exhaled, but nodded. Dammit. After what had happened with Charlie and with Riley, she longed to run back to her emotional cave. But the ache to have someone in her life pushed harder. "I just need to find the right guy."

"Are you sure you haven't?"

She wrinkled her nose in confusion. "Yes? I'm certain it's not Riley. Or Charlie."

Her mom shrugged and focused on her dinner. "If you say so. But I'll point out that your face really lit up when you were talking about Charlie."

She lifted her brows in a challenge, but her mom didn't glance her way. "No, Mama. Not Charlie."

13

Laurel pulled in front of Sagecreek Distillery a good ten minutes past the time scheduled to begin Afton's wedding rehearsal. She cursed as she exited her jeep and hurried to the restaurant's courtyard. She hated to be late.

If the editor at Pinecone's paper could put his ego away for a minute to give someone else a chance to speak, she wouldn't have had to fake a poor connection and hang up on him. He'd called back twice during her mad dash to the distillery, and she hadn't answered either time.

Phones lost reception all the time. Or batteries died. She'd apologize profusely for her phone's folly when she called him later. She'd smooth it on thick, and he'd eat it right up.

She hoped.

Regardless, this was her best friend's wedding rehearsal, and it took the top spot on her list of priorities. They'd waited until later in the evening to do the trial run because the pastor had a previous engagement. She didn't mind in the least. The temperature was perfect for a summer evening, with a soft breeze added to make it heavenly.

Laurel hurried toward the small crowd gathered in the lush courtyard just off the new restaurant.

Afton rolled her eyes in relief when she spotted her. "There you are. I was about to send out the cavalry."

She glanced at Corey and his father Martin, who would walk Afton down the aisle, and then Charlie caught her gaze. She should have looked away immediately, but she hadn't seen the man in over two weeks, not since her disastrous date with Riley, and he looked so good.

She gave him a slight smile, and then the pastor cleared his throat, drawing her attention. Still, she swore she could feel the heat of his gaze on the back of her head.

Pastor Bob was a mountain of a man, standing well over six feet and weighing twice what she did. His rounded belly matched his balding head, but his face carried the kindest smile.

"Thanks everyone for coming today. This shouldn't take long. We just need to do a quick run-through of the ceremony so that everyone knows what's expected come Saturday. Emotions will run high, so a little preparation goes a long way."

Laurel still couldn't believe her best friend would be married in four days. It all seemed so unreal, yet she couldn't be happier for her. Though Afton and Corey had come from vastly different backgrounds, they were perfect for each other.

"Afton, Martin, Laurel, and Charlie all need to head over to the restaurant entrance, where you'll be emerging for the ceremony. Corey, you'll stay here and wait for your bride."

Afton caught Laurel's attention and widened her eyes in nervous anticipation. She grinned in return. Their day would be so perfect. Laurel slipped her arm through Afton's and together they walked toward what would be their starting point, with the two men falling in a few steps behind them.

Afton leaned close. "I'm already so nervous. I'm afraid I'll fall apart on Saturday."

Laurel used her free hand to pat Afton's arm. "You're going to be the perfect bride, and it's going to be a perfect day. Don't worry. I'll be here for whatever you need."

She blinked back quick tears. "Thank you so much for that. You and your mom are really my only family." Afton's parents had dumped her on her grandpa's doorstep so many years ago and left him to raise her. And sadly, her grandpa had passed before Afton was even engaged.

"And now you'll have Corey's."

Afton exhaled and smiled. "Yes. They are wonderful people."

"You weren't able to locate your mom or dad?" Laurel asked.

She gave a quick shake of her head. "Decided I didn't want to. I'd wanted to invite them so that I could put things behind me and start with a fresh future." She sniffed. "Then I realized they'd done that very thing the day they walked out of my life. Johnnie Searle was mother, father and grandpa to me. He's the only one who counts, and I hate he won't be here."

They stopped at the entrance to the restaurant, and Laurel turned to her friend. "He'll be here, Afton. Right here." She made a fist over her heart.

She nodded and whispered, "Thank you."

The pastor brought the small group together to give them instructions. As he did, Laurel snuck glances at Charlie. She couldn't ignore the man or the sparks he generated, no matter how much she wished she could.

On the flip side, Charlie didn't seem to have a problem ignoring her at all. He didn't look in her direction until the pastor explained the two of them would lead the procession. Charlie gave her a friendly smile as though he'd just noticed her and held out his elbow for her. "This ought to be fun."

She slipped her hand around his bicep, her fingertips sizzling as they glided over his bare skin. All thoughts and sensations centered on the spot where they touched, and she tried to pretend that standing next to him wasn't enough to send her spiraling. Her pulse throbbed in wild beats, and she was certain her thumping heart was loud enough to give her away.

Afton and her future father-in-law assembled behind them.

"Wait here until I give you the cue." The pastor turned to walk away.

Laurel fought to tune out Charlie's presence, but it was an uphill battle on ice. Though in her mind, she knew he wasn't good for her, her body disagreed.

Charlie shifted his weight from foot to foot while they waited for the pastor to talk to Corey. Finally, Charlie released a deep exhale, causing her to look at him.

"What?" she asked.

"Nothing," he mumbled, and then glanced at Afton and Martin behind them.

Clearly, whatever he had to say, he didn't intend to say it in front of anyone. That or he used them as an excuse to cover whatever was tumbling in his mind. The pastor then called the group forward, and Charlie escorted her to where Corey waited for them.

Corey stared at Afton with a misty gaze. If he was this emotionally affected by the sight of her during rehearsal, she could only imagine how he'd be when they exchanged vows. Perhaps one day, she'd inspire a man to love her like that.

After the pastor walked them through their steps, he pulled Corey and Afton aside to discuss their intentions for their wedding vows.

Laurel wandered to a bench beneath a cluster of aspens where she'd wait to see if she needed to know anything else before she left. She'd barely sat down when Charlie headed in her direction. He'd done an excellent job of ignoring her as much as possible during the rehearsal, but he seemed to have other intentions now.

The man reminded her of the mountain lion she'd come across while trekking in the Wasatch Mountains the previous summer. She'd spotted the wild cat below the ridge where she hiked. It moved with an athletic grace that was beautiful and deadly at the same time. She'd thought to run then, as she did now, but she knew in her heart she could never look away from something so magnificent.

His eyes flashed with the interest she craved and had feared she'd lost as he sat beside her. "I haven't seen you around for a while."

"Yeah. Life's been busy." Which was a big lie. It wasn't that she didn't have work to do, but with him on her mind, she struggled to craft a decent sentence, making her job much harder.

He gazed across the courtyard at the happy couple. "Same."

"I'm sure, with you being so close to opening the restaurant."

He cast a quick sideways glance in her direction. "Exactly."

She hated that their conversation didn't flow like it normally did, and she knew she was to blame. "I wanted to apologize for Riley's rude behavior a few weeks ago."

"That's right. You had a date with him."

As if either of them had forgotten the awkward encounter.

He lifted his chin. "No need for you to apologize. You weren't the jerk."

"Asshole is more like it," she said under her breath.

Charlie choked on a laugh and then cleared his throat. "Why don't you tell me how you really feel?" he teased.

"You know I'm right."

He ran a thumb over the rough wooden armrest on the bench, keeping his focus there. "Can't argue with you about that. What I wondered was why you'd date him in the first place. He doesn't seem like your type."

"Why do you say that?" He didn't know her *type*. She wasn't even sure she did. "He's strong and steady. If he wasn't such a jerk, he might have been perfect."

Charlie snorted. "He's way too tame for you, not to mention an asshole."

"What's wrong with tame?" Didn't most people want a quiet, normal future?

He slid a sideways glance toward her. "Don't tell me you don't enjoy excitement in your life."

Excitement like the night he'd kissed her? Her heart stumbled at the thought of Charlie's lips on hers. "You don't know what you're talking about."

"I don't, *Miss Penn*?"

Curses rolled through her mind. So what if he'd taken the time to figure out her alias? Meant nothing. "Besides, Riley wasn't my choice. My mom set me up with him."

He straightened. "He didn't ask you out?"

She shook her head.

The corner of his mouth tilted in a quick grin and then disappeared just as fast. A small tell? Had she made him jealous? She pondered the idea for a moment and realized she liked it.

Realistically though, he had to have twenty girls on the side ready to steal his attention if she wasn't interested. She doubted she'd triggered jealousy unless his ego was at stake. Some guys were like that.

Afton and Corey broke from the pastor and strode toward them, hand in hand. Laurel couldn't say she'd witnessed a cuter couple.

Corey nodded to Charlie. "Mind giving me a lift home? Afton needs to wrap up a few details tonight, and I'm meeting with the other council members at seven."

"No problem." Charlie stood and then glanced down at her. "Guess I'll see you on Saturday."

She smiled, missing him before he even walked away. "See you Saturday." Why couldn't she convince her heart to forget him?

Laurel and Afton remained silent as the two men walked away. "Best guys I know," Afton said with much affection.

"You and Corey are lucky to have each other. I'm beginning to believe love like yours doesn't happen often."

Afton gave her a soft smile. "It will happen for you. I used to think the same thing, that there was no one out there who would get me, but now look."

She snorted softly. "You deserve it more than anyone I know."

"So do you." Her friend exhaled and glanced across the courtyard.

Most of the trees and gardens were new. With time, it would become a beautiful setting for outdoor dining when the temperatures allowed. The view of the rolling hills and mountains beyond instilled a sense of peace and contentment that Laurel craved. "If I ever find someone to marry, I think I'd like to have my wedding here as well. The scenery is stunning."

"That's a great idea. I should talk to Charlie about expanding our services once his restaurant is up and running. There's no reason we couldn't host all kinds of special events out here in the courtyard." Afton elbowed her. "Thanks for that smart tip. Multiple income streams are the way to go."

She beamed. "No problem. I wish I was as good at sorting out my life as I am yours."

"That's why we're best friends, to tell each other the shit

we're too blind to see." Afton paused. "Such as how much Charlie likes you."

Laurel narrowed her gaze to argue the point, but she couldn't keep a smile from popping on her lips. "He likes all women."

"Not the way he likes you."

Afton's revelation coursed through her like warm honey, and she struggled not to lap up every drop. "He's a wildcard at best."

Her friend scoffed. "Why are you so hard on the guy? He hasn't dated another woman since you went out, and it's not that he hasn't had the chance. I know Mallory flirts with him relentlessly every time she sees him. Then there's Lexie, who thinks he's a god, but he doesn't look twice. Every day we're here, he brings your name into the conversation. That date you had with Riley sure threw him for a loop. He stormed around here like a thundercloud after he'd seen you together. I think the poor guy is hopelessly besotted with you."

"*Besotted?*" She rolled her eyes. They couldn't be talking about the same man. "If he missed me so much, then why hasn't he called?" There. She'd said it. She'd wondered about him so many times over the past two weeks, but she hadn't seen or heard from him.

"He's afraid. But don't you dare tell him I said so. He would flat out filet me and fry me up for dinner."

"Afraid?" That made no sense. "*Of me?*"

"Afraid of scaring you off. Afraid you're not interested in the least. You're the wild card, Laurel. The one woman not affected by his charms."

"I wouldn't say I'm not affected," she mumbled.

Afton laughed. "I knew it. You can deny it all you want, and he can pretend to ignore it, but when the two of you are in the same vicinity, sparks fly like fireworks on the Fourth of July."

She shifted to face her friend directly. "You're exaggerating."

"The hell I am. Everyone can see it but you, Laurel. You both like each other, and you're both good people. Why don't you give it a chance?"

She held up a hand before Laurel could reply. "I've heard your objections a million times, and I don't buy them. Stop being so stubborn and bull-headed, and date the man. Quit dancing around each other and give the relationship a shot. You might be surprised at the gem hiding inside."

Laurel's nerves tingled as though lightning bugs jigged inside her. "I don't know." She'd thought she would instantly know when she met the right man for her. But what if she was wrong?

"For hell's sake, Laurel. You're one of the bravest women I know. Stop acting like a coward. I'm not going to say that psycho Abercrombie hasn't had the hugest impact on you. I know I haven't been there and don't know what it's like to come back from something like that. But it is what it is. It's a part of who you are, but don't let it be all you are."

Afton exhaled a deep breath. "You want something special in your life? Then don't be afraid to take a chance. You've given your past far too much control over your life. It's time to leave that in the dust once and for all."

Only Afton could talk to her that way. But she was right. She knew if she didn't follow her heart this time, she'd regret it for the rest of her life. She had to stop being scared. Even if Charlie gave her the greatest heartbreak of all time, she had to know.

The *what if* question had reached critical mass.

She had to know.

14

Laurel checked her hair and makeup one last time in the full-length mirror Afton had installed in her office, while Afton retrieved the jeweled hairpiece she'd chosen to wear instead of a veil. The office wasn't the greatest dressing room ever, but with only the two of them, they made it work. With soft music playing, the room had a cozy, relaxed feel.

Laurel's lavender chiffon dress complimented her hair perfectly and darkened her eyes to a rich coffee color. Soft ruffles at her shoulders left her arms bare and traveled to a deep vee in front. The satin sash around her waist flattered her curves and added an extra touch of class. She wasn't sure if she'd ever felt this pretty in her entire life.

Of course, she paled compared to Afton's stunning princess gown made with an off-white lace bodice and layers of tulle for the skirt. She didn't mind. This was her friend's day, and she was determined it would be perfect.

Afton came into view in the mirror behind her, and they both smiled. "You're so beautiful, Laurel."

She laughed. "I'm nothing compared to you. Sit down in this chair and let me help you."

The bride held still while Laurel wove the string of jewels throughout her friend's updo. The crystals and pearls nestled against her strands, making her look every bit the fairy princess. "You're so stunning that I think I might cry." Emotion welled in her throat, and she laughed at her silly behavior.

"If you cry, I'm going to cry, and then we'll both ruin our makeup and have to start all over, which will make for some unhappy guests."

Laurel sniffed and caught Afton's reflection in the mirror. "You're right. No tears. At least not until after the ceremony. After that, all bets are off."

Ten minutes later, she and Afton left her office together and headed down the hall that led to the restaurant entrance. Heavenly scents from the baby pink roses filled the mostly empty room, while sparkling lights glittered overhead. Corey's dad and Charlie stood by the door leading to the courtyard and looked up as they made their way across the room. Martin smiled, but the look of utter appreciation on Charlie's face stole her breath. He didn't glance at Afton one time. Instead, he focused on her with a smoldering gaze, making her feel she might spontaneously combust.

The gray tailored suit he wore, accented by a lavender bowtie, created a dashing, handsome and sexy visual that heated her blood. When they neared, Charlie stepped forward and took her hand.

Keeping his gaze locked with hers, he brought her hand to his lips and kissed. Crazy tingles sizzled in her blood, but she couldn't look away. "You are quite possibly the most beautiful woman I've ever seen."

She fought to breathe.

Martin snorted. "I thought that was what the groom was supposed to say to the bride."

Charlie still didn't look away. "He better hope he does, or he'll be in a boatload of trouble if he can't measure up to the best man."

He finally blinked and shifted his gaze toward Afton. A warm smile spread across his lips and resonated deep in Laurel's heart. It was clear he cared deeply about her best friend. He leaned in and kissed her on the cheek. "Corey is a lucky man."

Afton returned his affectionate gesture. "Thank you. All of you for being here to share this day with us. You're my family, and I'm blessed to have such wonderful people in my life."

Tears of happiness welled behind Laurel's eyes, and she quickly blinked them away. Neither she nor Afton had much family if they only counted blood relatives, but they had each other and a wonderful, supportive community.

Laurel's mom poked her head inside the doors and glanced at each person. "Looks like you're ready. We'll cue the music."

Laurel fussed with the train on Afton's gown, gave her a quick kiss on the cheek, and took her place at the front of the procession.

Charlie's engaging smile generated another wave of nervous energy. "Ready?" he asked.

Ready for the wedding? "Yes." Ready for what came next in her life? Not so much.

The doors to the courtyard swung open, and she slid her arm around his. Electricity popped and sparked in her veins. Being near him never failed to send her reality spinning wildly out of control.

Laurel held back her tears as the couple exchanged vows, but the moment Pastor Bob pronounced them man and wife, several slid down her cheek. She was utterly and completely happy for her friend, and she craved what they'd found with every inch of her being. She ached for someone to look at her like that, for someone who'd pledge his life to her. Something so permanent seemed incredibly out of reach, but many found it every day.

Was it so hard to believe that if she put herself out there, she could find the same?

A crowd of people swelled around the newlyweds to offer congratulations, and Laurel stepped aside to make room.

Charlie joined her. "They make a great couple."

She smiled and nodded. "They do."

Laurel shifted her gaze from Afton and Corey to Charlie. As hard as she tried to keep her walls between them in place, he blasted them to pieces with one devastating smile.

He narrowed his gaze. "What?"

She blinked, suddenly aware she stared. "What?" she tossed back for lack of anything else to say.

"You were looking at me funny."

Her pulse rate increased tenfold. "No, I wasn't. My mind drifted, and I was thinking."

"About?" he prompted.

Dear God, help her. "What amazing things you might have cooked for the reception dinner."

His eyes sparkled with amusement. "Something incredibly delicious that will please all your senses."

Of that, she had no doubt. "I'm looking forward to it."

"So am I."

Those eyes. The way he could stare straight into her soul stole her breath. She should look away, but she found she didn't want to. She liked the way she felt when he focused on her, liked the way his attention spun a web of intimacy between them, even though many others surrounded them.

As much as she fought it, her attraction to Charlie Blackmore had increased exponentially.

Charlie broke their connection first when he shifted his gaze beyond her. "Hey there."

Lexie joined them, looking confident and sexy in a short navy sundress. Her long blond curls cascaded over one shoulder, and her lips were a perfect siren red.

"Hello, Charlie." She cast a quick glance at Laurel before she dismissed her. "I wanted to offer my congratulations on the grand opening of your new restaurant."

He dipped his head in gracious acknowledgement. "I was just telling Laurel that I have something spectacular planned for tonight's meal. Something to entice everyone to come back again and again."

She touched his forearm for a moment. "I'm sure you'll have no problem with that."

Laurel arched her brow. That was a come-on if she'd ever seen one, and that irritated her more than dirt in her eyes on a windy day. One thing was for sure. She wouldn't compete for Charlie's attention.

She took a step back. "I'm going to head inside."

Before she could leave, Charlie grasped her hand, stopping her. "Hang on, Laurel. Lexie, I hope you enjoy your meal. Thanks again for the congratulations. I'd love to know what you think of our offerings."

Lexie didn't spare her a glance. "Of course. And you're busy with your best man duties right now. I won't keep you. Maybe one day next week, I'll drop by to say hello."

"I'll most likely be here, so don't bother coming to the house."

Why was he still holding her hand if he wanted to encourage Lexie? She wished she could jerk away and flee inside. She didn't need to witness this.

Hell. Was his goal to make her jealous?

"Okay." Lexie gave him a small, flirty wave. "I'll see you later."

Laurel rolled her eyes and pulled from him, making her way to the restaurant door.

Charlie caught up with her in time to open it for her. "We're over here." With a warm hand on her back, he guided her through the empty room lit with soft hanging light bulbs and twinkling lights to the bridal party table at the head of the room. Bouquets of baby pink roses graced the center of each table and infused the room with a lovely scent.

"Thank you," she said stiffly as he slid out a chair for her.

"She's nothing to me, Laurel," he whispered near her shoulder, and she was embarrassed that he'd read her so well.

"Then why do you flirt with her like that?" Her question was out before she could stop herself.

He squatted next to her chair so his face was on the same level as hers. "Because Lexie and her large, extensive family are potential customers. I'll need as many people in here as I can get to keep this thing afloat, and it doesn't hurt to be nice."

She wasn't buying it. "There's nice, and then there's *nice*."

A deep, sexy chuckle rumbled from his chest. "I'm going to get us champagne, lovely lady. There is too much happiness today to let one flirtatious, pushy woman ruin it for us." He grinned as he stood and then strode away.

She watched him leave, her pulse thumping wildly inside her. Dammit. She needed to stop acting like a jealous teenager. She was a grown woman with an amazing career that she loved. She didn't need a man. Certainly didn't need Charlie. She'd known from the beginning he was a ladies' man and would be nothing but trouble. She couldn't complain now.

Charlie could date whomever he liked. One kiss between them meant nothing.

"Here we go."

The sound of Charlie's magnetic voice drew her attention, and she looked up to find him holding two full glasses. He held one out to her, and she took it.

Instead of sitting, he leaned close to her so that she had to tilt her head and look over her shoulder to see him.

His face hovered inches from hers, and her body danced with excitement ignited by his proximity. "Did I mention how beautiful you look this evening?"

She swallowed as she struggled to maintain her thoughts. What was the man playing at? "Yes. Thank you." Her heartbeats roared.

He placed a finger beneath her chin to ensure she held his gaze. "The kitchen help needs me for a few minutes."

"Okay." She could use a break from his overwhelming presence, anyway.

He studied her eyes for a long moment and then lowered his head toward hers and placed a quick, but heated kiss on her lips. He took one sip of his champagne before setting his glass on the table. Then he strode away.

He'd done it again.

She placed her fingertips to lips that still sizzled. That was the second time he'd stolen a kiss without asking. The second time that he'd tipped her world upside down and left her to deal with the aftermath.

She wrapped her fingers around the stem of her wineglass and drank. Commotion drew her attention, and she spotted Afton walking toward her with a beautiful, glowing look on her face.

"Saw that." Afton winked.

Heat blossomed on her cheeks. She closed her eyes and shook her head.

Afton claimed a seat next to her. "What's the problem? He's

handsome. You're gorgeous. You're both the best people I know. You seem to be perfect for each other."

That Charlie might be the one for her only increased her anxiety. "Stop saying that."

Afton studied her with a sincere look. "Do you want me to tell him to back off? Because I will. If you truly aren't interested, just let me know."

If she did that, she'd be lying. "I...He... He scares the hell out of me. He's too kind. Too handsome."

Her friend released a soft chuckle. "He has the power to break your heart."

"Yes," she said with a gasp.

Afton took her hand and squeezed. "Those are the ones worth dating. You're wasting your time otherwise."

The rest of the bridal party approached the table, cutting short their conversation. Afton passed her a smile that said they'd talk later.

15

Laurel discovered if a person drank enough wine at her best friend's wedding, she could drown her fears until they were nothing but quiet whispers. After a few glasses, she found it easier to laugh with the wedding group, and when Charlie asked her to dance later, she had no qualms about saying yes.

After even more wine, they owned the dance floor. In fact, she and Charlie might have given the bride and groom a run for their money.

But having a good time also equated to time racing away at a record speed. Before Laurel knew it, many of the single women in town had lined up to catch the bride's bouquet.

"Why aren't you vying for her flowers?" Charlie whispered in her ear, sending another round of shivers skittering through her. She couldn't deny he'd ensnared her with his charms. Right now, she didn't care. She loved to catch him staring at her. Loved the way he'd awakened a longing inside her she hadn't known existed. He made her feel more alive than any of the adventurous things she'd done in her life.

"It's a silly tradition," she said. "Besides, it doesn't work, anyway. I've witnessed Sally Hall catch more than one bouquet, and she's been single for years."

As she turned to watch the festivities, she widened her eyes in dismay. Oh, God. That could be her in a few years. Alone. Always searching. Never finding.

It wouldn't be a horrible way to live, but it wasn't what she wanted.

"Laurel," Afton called and nodded toward the assembly of women.

She smiled and shook her head, earning a frown from Afton. The bride turned her back. She glanced once more over her shoulder and then tossed.

Her bouquet hit Laurel smack in the chest, and she gasped in surprise. Charlie caught the flowers before they fell to the floor. He met her gaze with a smile that left her breathless.

He held them out to her. "Looks like they were meant for you."

She snorted. "Afton aimed for me."

He released a soft chuckle that burrowed its way into her core. "No one can aim that precisely when tossing backward over one's head."

Knowing Afton, she wouldn't bet on that.

Laurel waited until the bride and groom departed before she thought to find her mother. "Have you seen my mom?" she asked Charlie.

"She left a while ago. Said she was tired. I offered to give you a ride home, and she was grateful. I was supposed to tell you she said she'd stop by your house and check on the pets."

His words shocked her. "Was my mom okay with that?"

He shrugged. "Why wouldn't she be?"

Okay, then... "Thank you," she said instead. The thought of having someone take care of her was nice, and if her mom wasn't freaking out, she certainly wouldn't either.

As he escorted her to his truck, a quiet voice nagged at her. *What was she doing with this guy? Could he really like her? Should she give him a chance? Why was she so certain he wasn't the one?*

Laughing and dancing with him tonight had been incredible, and she knew one thing. *She wanted more.*

After settling her into the passenger seat, he climbed into the driver's side and devastated her with another engaging smile. "Thanks for hanging out with me tonight. I had a great time."

A smile blossomed on her lips. "Me, too. It was an amazing evening, and I'm sorry it's over."

He glanced over his shoulder before pulling onto the lane that would take them back to the main road. "Same. I'm going to have a hard time sleeping tonight. Too much energy."

Exactly. "It's because Afton and Corey have the best friends and family."

"Us included," he added with a smile.

"Of course. With so many loving and supportive people around, it creates that kind of positive energy."

"Agreed." He drummed his fingers on the steering wheel. "You know, I hate to say it, but I almost didn't come to Aspen that night we first met. Corey always bragged about his little town while we were in college, and he'd invited me many times before, but I'd always blown him off."

The thought that they might have never met bothered her. As much as he drove her crazy, if she didn't have him interrupting every other thought in her head, her life would be boring. "What finally made you decide to visit?"

He stopped at the end of the lane, glanced for oncoming traffic, which was highly unlikely even in the busiest daytime hours, and then pulled onto the main road. "My dad was being a dick, harassing me about coming back to the family business, and I'd had enough. It was a Friday night, so I packed a bag and headed out of town. I figured a quick road trip would help me get my head on straight."

She studied his profile while he spoke and basked in the deep timbres of his voice.

He snorted. "Funny thing about that. After being here for the weekend, I realized my head was just fine. It's the people in my family who are messed up. I come from a long line of workaholics who end up drinking too much and will probably die young from all the stress. Sure, they have the money and lifestyle that go with it, but anyone can see they're not happy."

She pictured an ornery group of people. "Money is only worth so much."

He shot a quick glance in her direction and smiled as though he was pleased she'd agreed with him. "I'm glad I took a chance and followed my heart."

A burst of warmth rushed through her. "Me, too."

"I've always admired Corey, but I couldn't ask for a better business partner than Afton. She's a hell of a lady. Knows exactly what she wants, and she isn't afraid to go for it."

"Yeah, she's amazing. She had to fight for every bit of it, though. Her feisty grandfather was an enormous influence up until..." The memory of that horrific day the world lost Johnny Searle still clogged her throat with emotion.

He nodded in understanding. "Afton told me the story. She talks about him a lot, about the original distillery he kept hidden in the hills. I keep asking her to show me, but we haven't had much downtime during the past few months."

"I could show you." The offer was out of her mouth like a bullet from a trigger-happy teenager's rifle.

"Yeah?" He cast a quick glance in her direction as though checking her sincerity. "I'd really like that. But don't tease me like Afton and make me wait forever."

Her pulse increased, her heart running rampant in her

chest. Decisions were much easier now that she'd decided to give him a chance. "How about now?" Her mind stuttered over what her heart had just said.

"Now?" He seemed as surprised by her offer as she was.

She shrugged. Afton was right. Flirting could be fun. Addictive, even. "You have a four-wheel drive. As long as you know how to drive your truck, we shouldn't have any problems."

A wicked grin tilted his lips. "Oh, darlin'. I know how to drive this truck."

Her insane heart stomped her thoughts into submission, urging her onward. "The moon is full, and I have a flashlight on my phone so we can see our way around. Unless you'd rather wait for daylight."

She hoped he agreed to go, because she didn't want to wait. She wanted this night to go on forever. More than that, she wanted to throw caution to the wind and kiss Charlie again.

He slowed and then swung his truck around on the highway. "This is happening."

She swallowed and hung onto the seat as he made the sharp turn. *Yes, it was.* She'd stepped a little farther out of her shell and couldn't be happier. Afton was right. If she wanted a different life. She had to be brave enough to make different choices. And tonight, at this moment, she was ready to take a chance on Charlie.

Charlie followed her directions, and soon his truck bounced over the rutted trail that carried them along uneven earth and rocks. She managed lighthearted conversation, but anticipation built as the truck climbed the hillside.

He stopped when they came to the edge of the river. "Now what?"

She grinned, feeling sassy. She realized that some loss of her inhibitions came from consuming champagne. But she knew it was mostly because she'd been in sync with Charlie all night, leaving her wonderfully lighthearted. "I thought you said you could drive this thing. We go through it, of course."

He held her gaze for a long moment and then laughed. "Okay. I'll trust you on this one." Slow and easy, he made his way to the other side.

"It's more fun to go fast."

He snorted. "Is that so? And this is coming from a woman who has no fun?"

"Whatever." She rolled her eyes, enjoying their carefree jaunt up the hill. "Afton told me she'd mentioned the type of articles I write, so I think you know my life isn't too boring."

He grinned as he kept his gaze on the dirt trail ahead of them. "Oh, darlin'. Boring is a word I'd never use when talking about you."

Why, oh why, had she held Charlie at bay for so long? She'd made herself miserable and had missed out on all this fun.

They neared the once-hidden opening that led to the old distillery. "Her grandfather used to camouflage this turnoff with potted trees and tree branches to camouflage the pots, if you can believe that. He'd move them when he needed to enter, but no one ever caught on to his scheme except Afton. Several had tried to bust him, but he was a smart man."

"Like his granddaughter," Charlie said.

"Exactly." She pointed up ahead. "See the cave entrance? You can park near there."

Fresh scents of pine and earth greeted her as Charlie helped her out of the truck. She stepped carefully until she was assured the ground was hard enough that her heels wouldn't sink in.

Without the headlights from the truck, mystical shadows ruled, but the bright moon compensated just enough to make it romantic. A soft wind blew her skirt about her legs, and she inhaled deeply. "I loved the party, but it's nice to be away from everyone, too. I think better when I'm in places like this."

He lifted his brows in a teasing manner. "Planning on doing a lot of thinking tonight, are you?"

She chuckled at the absurdity of his question. "No." Then she caught his gaze and held it. A heady surge of power fed her courage. "I'm not planning on thinking at all."

His lips slid into a grin that stole her breath. "I like that idea."

She meant it. No questioning. No wondering. For once, she intended to follow her heart and see where it took her. If she could live fearlessly in her professional life, she could in her personal life, too.

She linked her fingers with his and held tight. If her actions surprised him, he didn't show it. "Come on. There's not much left of the distillery anymore, but you can still get a sense of what it must have been like before the accident."

"Let's do it." Charlie twisted his fingers until his hand completely engulfed hers and their connection was solid. She smiled as she continued to lead the way. At the entrance to the cave, she paused long enough to turn on her phone's flashlight.

Shadows danced on the walls, escaping the light as she and Charlie stepped over piles of rubble. "Nothing was visible from the outside back then, either. If a person peeked into this cave, he would see nothing but rock."

"Smart thinking."

She moved deeper inside and then came to a stop. "Here's where he stored everything. When Afton discovered this place, she said she'd found hundreds of bottles of illegal, highly potent Sagecreek Whiskey ready for sale. Everyone in town loved it. They called it the best whiskey around. Afton uses the same recipe, but somehow it doesn't taste the same, knowing it's not bootleg whiskey."

He laughed. "Maybe because danger has a way of heightening senses."

She glanced at him, tightening the tension between them. "Do you like to live dangerously, Charlie?"

"Sometimes." He held her gaze for a long, heart-stopping moment. "The question is, do you?"

He'd turned that on her so fast her head spun. "Occasionally." Like right now.

She was certain he'd kiss her then. But he didn't, and the dim light from her phone did little to illuminate his face, making it hard to read his expression.

Tension needled her to the point she found it hard to think. "Her grandpa kept a trailer up here. I believe Afton hasn't moved it. I think she comes here when she needs solitude or wants to feel close to her grandpa. It's not far if you don't mind a short walk."

"You're not really dressed for hiking," he said as he followed her out of the cave.

She glanced over her shoulder as they emerged. "There's a trail. I'll be fine."

And she was. Mostly. She stumbled once on a protruding rock, but Charlie was quick to wrap an arm around her waist to steady her. Only problem was, the feel of his hand just above her hip with only the thin fabric of her dress separating them sent her pulse racing worse than it already was.

A small, white trailer nestled in the trees came into view, and Laurel stopped at the edge of a circle of stones near a large log that had been fashioned into a bench. "Looks like they've cleared away a few of the trees, and I know this fire pit wasn't here the last time I was."

Charlie moved in next to her, his body close enough she could feel his heat. With the chilly temperatures and the aching in her heart, she wished she could move closer. "Maybe she and Corey use it as a getaway," Charlie suggested.

"You're probably right." She snorted. "This was the first

place they'd…" She caught herself before she divulged Afton's private information.

Charlie squeezed her hand, forcing her to look at him. "They'd what, Laurel?"

She swallowed as embarrassed heat climbed her cheeks. "You know, made love."

A smile crossed his lips and left a tremble in her heart. "I see. It is a romantic spot."

"Uh-huh." She willed him to lower his lips to hers, prayed for him to take her in his arms. But he didn't move.

He also didn't look away.

Her breath caught in her throat as delicious tension built between them. She imagined slipping her arms over those broad shoulders and pulling him in for a kiss. The waiting and wondering nearly did her in.

"Aren't you going to kiss me?" she asked before she burst with anticipation.

"Do you want me to?" His low voice echoed through the silent evening.

"Yes," she whispered.

She'd beg if she had to.

16

Gently, Charlie took Laurel's face between his hands, searching her eyes for several long moments. Tender love floated in his expression, swirling her fragile feelings. He brushed a thumb across her lips, casting shivers through her entire body. She tried to breathe, but it was hard to do anything other than stare into his adoring eyes.

She sucked in a shaky breath as Charlie leaned closer. The moment his lips touched hers, a rush of sensations and emotion swept her away. Her insides curled in on themselves before bursting outward like rays of brilliant sunshine.

Unable to help herself, she leaned into him, allowing him to explore with his kisses, cherishing each second of the delicious connection.

His kiss lingered long on her lips, and Laurel savored each moment. Though his touch was gentle, she also sensed a fierceness and possessiveness that knocked her off balance. She wanted whatever it was between them to be right.

In her heart, he felt right. But what if she was wrong?

She pulled back, her breaths coming hard, and stepped

away from him with a laugh. "Wow." She swallowed. "That was amazing. You must have had a lot of practice."

He studied her as though looking for the underlying meaning of her words. "Some, but nothing compares to kissing you."

Her breath whooshed from her lungs. "Good answer." But could she believe it?

He closed the distance between them and took her hand, but he made no move to push further. "It's the truth."

He pinned her with his gaze for several unnerving moments, and she swore unseen threads bound them together. Then he surprised her by breaking their connection to survey the surrounding clearing instead. "Looks like they have plenty of firewood. What do you say we warm ourselves?"

She hadn't sat around a campfire for years, and the idea appealed to her romantic side immensely. "Okay. But you'll need matches or a lighter, too. So, unless you have one in your truck, we might be out of luck."

He snorted. "Woman of little faith. Just so you know, I don't need a lighter or matches."

She narrowed her eyes in doubt, but grinned. "You can't be serious."

"Oh, I am. Watch and learn, darlin'."

Darlin'? His words spilled sweetly from his lips and wove his web tighter.

He left her standing by the lifeless fire pit while he strode back to his truck. He returned a minute later with a blanket. He also held up a tiny baggie for her inspection. "Flint and steel, and something for us to sit on instead of the bare log."

She spread the folded blanket over the log bench. "Better hurry," she teased. "I'm getting cold. I might use this blanket to keep me warm instead."

His sexy chuckle vibrated the air around them. "Oh, hell no. It's not going to be that blanket that keeps you warm."

She held his gaze and shivered.

"Shine your phone over by the trailer."

As she did, he gathered a few smaller pieces of wood from the pile nearby and then swiped a handful of dead grass before he returned. Kneeling, he assembled the items before him.

"You're going to ruin your nice clothes," she warned.

"Anything to keep you warm," he said without looking up.

She rolled her eyes. The man sure knew how to lay it on thick. Still, she loved his charming words.

Charlie worked for a few minutes, scraping the flint down the side of the steel toward a nest of grass to generate sparks. He repeated his movements several times before he stopped and blew ever so softly on the nest. A flame caught hold, and she inhaled in delight.

He carefully set the nest of burning grass into the fire pit and added twigs and more grass. Before long, the flames grew brighter, their light bouncing off the trees.

She never would have believed it. "I'm impressed."

He stood and added a few larger logs to the fire before he brushed off his hands and pants. "That's my goal. To impress you." He strode to the log bench and sat next to her, making her shiver.

"Warm enough?"

She glanced at him from the corner of her eye, not daring to look at him directly, and smiled. "I'm getting there."

He scooted a little closer and wrapped his arm around her shoulder, generating more sparks. "How about now?"

"Yes," she said. "I'm definitely warmer now." The feel of his hard, strong body next to hers seemed so right.

His smile crinkled the corners of his eyes, and he shifted his gaze to the crackling fire. "You know, Laurel, I've been thinking about you a lot, and I believe I've figured you out."

He'd been thinking about her? A lot? "You have?"

"Mm-hmm. You're not all that complicated. You want to take chances and live life to the fullest. You've done it in other areas of your life, but the final frontier is your heart. Untamed, unexplored territory."

She inhaled sharply. Afton must have told him something.

He shifted toward her. "Am I wrong?"

She took a moment to answer. "No. Not exactly."

She'd never boiled down her feelings so succinctly, but he was right. So right. She didn't ask for what had happened to her, but she was left to try to have a good life despite it.

"That's it? You're not going to argue with me?"

She had nothing to argue about. "No," she whispered.

Her answer seemed to catch him off guard as well, and he studied her with a look that sent her heart racing into overdrive. After a moment, he gave her a slight nod. "Okay. Then I'm going to go one further. You're not afraid to date men. You're just afraid to date me. And it's not because you don't like me."

Ah, hell. She remained quiet, praying he wouldn't hear the desperate beat of her heart as she searched for a response.

He tilted his head and looked at her earnestly. "Why, Laurel? Why are you so afraid of me?"

His question inflamed the war that had been raging inside her for a long time. She wanted to tell him, but she feared she'd become more vulnerable if she did.

He skimmed over the sensitized skin on her shoulder, sending a low tremble through her, cracking the surface of her defenses. He narrowed his eyes as though the action might help him read her mind. "You want someone safe?"

God, he could read her so well. She nodded.

"And I'm not safe."

"You scare the hell out of me," she said, her voice breathless.

He paused and then slowly shook his head. "You wouldn't be happy with safe. Not for long anyway."

"I might," she countered.

He trapped her gaze with intense eyes. "You can trust me. I would never want to hurt you."

She studied him in the flickering firelight, wishing with all her heart that she could know the truth.

"You have to know, Laurel, I wouldn't let you fall if I didn't intend to catch you."

Fall? As in love? Could she trust them both enough to find out what that might be like? Her gaze fell to his lips, and she swallowed.

He cupped her face, forcing her to look at him. "I'm not going to lie. I've wanted you from the first moment I saw you. But this is more than lust. Can't you feel it?"

He took her hand and held her palm against his chest. "Open your heart, Laurel. *Feel it.*"

Oh, God, she did. She felt everything he said and more. The way they laughed together. The way he read her mind. The way her whole body came alive whenever he was close to her.

But...

———

Charlie wished he knew what the hell to say to Laurel to crack open her shell once and for all. He sensed something held her back, but he'd be damned if he could figure out that much. "Do you really have such a low opinion of me?" It was the only reason he could fathom.

Laurel blinked a few times and then broke their connection, choosing to stare into the fire instead. "It's not you. It's me."

He expelled a sarcastic snort, frustrated as hell with her stupid walls. "Oh. The old, it's not you, it's me routine."

She turned back to him and studied him with a piercing look. "It really is, Charlie. I..." Her loud exhale washed into the night. "The truth is, if you knew everything, you probably wouldn't want to date me. I'm not your average girl."

He tightened his grip on her shoulder, afraid she'd bolt, though really, she had nowhere to go. "I can see that already. You're far beyond average."

She gave a small smile that encouraged him. "Beyond average in craziness, maybe."

He shifted, angling toward her. With his free hand, he took her fingers and squeezed, hoping to reassure her. "You're beyond anything I've ever imagined."

She tilted her head back, facing the night sky. "Don't say that. I'm..."

Whatever it was, he needed to know. "You obviously have something you need to say."

She faced him again, her eyes wide.

"Do you trust me enough to tell me that much? I'm a good listener, Laurel." *Please God, let her trust him*. He'd never find his way into her heart if she didn't.

"I have some issues."

He nodded. He'd gathered that much.

"Something happened to me years ago. Something that's bad...but not as bad as it could have been." Her voice grew quieter, and she shifted her gaze to the fire. "But apparently, I have trouble leaving it in the past. I'm doing my best, but it's hard sometimes."

"You can tell me, Laurel." He hugged her tighter against him. "I'd like to help if I can."

A long stretch of silence fell between them, punctuated only by the crackling and pops of the fire. When she finally spoke, her voice was subdued. "My mother went back to nursing school when I was nine. She also worked full time."

He nodded. She'd already told him that much. "That must have been tough for you."

She sighed. "It was. She was always at work by the time I got home from school. I missed having her there. Not that I blame her. My mom is a fighter, and she did what she had to do to make sure we had a place to live and food to eat. But—"

Her voice cracked, and the sound ripped through him.

She blew out a breath and tried to laugh. "I can't believe this is so hard. It's not the first time I've told anyone."

He caressed her shoulder. "Maybe because it's still a painful subject for you?"

She nodded and sniffed, leaving him with a heap of guilt for making her cry. "A few days before my tenth birthday, I was at the neighbor's house sitting on the porch doing homework, just like I did every day after school. The Abercrombie's watched me until my mom got home."

"That was nice of them," he encouraged.

Her half-laugh came out strangled, and she covered her mouth with the backs of her fingers. He ached to ease her anguish, but he had no idea how. Several long moments passed before she spoke again.

"That day was different. Mrs. Abercrombie had to leave for a doctor's appointment in town, so it was just me and her husband. I didn't mind. He'd always been very nice to me. We went inside the house where he fixed me a nice bowl of ice cream. I thought I was in heaven. My mom could rarely afford it, so it was a treat."

He slid his hand around hers and squeezed. When she rewarded him with a small smile, the tension inside him dropped a notch.

"Then he thought I might like a walk. He knew this cool

place not far into the hills. It had a little cabin, and lots of stuff to see along the way. Sounded like a fun adventure, so we took off. I didn't worry about letting my mom know or leaving a note for Mrs. Abercrombie. I wasn't even ten yet. Mr. Abercrombie was in charge, so I assumed it would be okay."

Damn, he wished he could see where she was going with her story. His brain whisked through multiple scenarios, and none of them were good.

"I had fun. We picked up cool rocks and talked about the different trees. The little shack looked like it had been there a long time. We went inside. It was dark and musty. Cobwebs everywhere. He told me a crazy man once lived there."

She paused to exhale. "I remember thinking I didn't like it there. It was creepy, and I wanted to leave. That's when Mr. Abercrombie knocked me to the ground."

Oh, God. "*No*." The one scenario he couldn't bear to consider.

She met his gaze, hers filled with anguish. "He held me down while he wrapped duct tape around my wrists. Then he lifted me to my feet and told me he was sorry. He didn't like to hurt me, but he needed me to mind him. I remember crying and him taking a piece of candy and sticking it in my mouth to help me quiet down."

"Laurel..." He pulled her tightly against him, tucking her head beneath his chin, and held her like he'd never let go.

"He locked me in the dirt cellar with a little lantern and told me he'd return. Everything after that is a blur. I know I cried, and I screamed, and I prayed. I think my mind tuned out many things to protect me."

She rested her head against his chest and slid her arms around him, and he hoped he brought her comfort. "It's not that bad," she whispered.

"How can you say that?" *How could she?*

"Beyond that, he never hurt me. He didn't get the chance. The police somehow broke him down during questioning, and he confessed to kidnapping me. When the police arrived, I freaked out, thinking it was Abercrombie, but they were there to rescue me."

"Oh, my God. *Thank God.*" That freak hadn't touched this lovely lady. "That could have turned out..." He couldn't finish his sentence.

She inhaled on a sob. "It did. For others. They didn't find only me in that cellar. He'd buried three other girls near where he'd tied me up." Her body shuddered with another sob. "I lived. They didn't."

He reached into his jacket pocket and pulled out the small pack of tissues Afton and Corey had given out at the wedding. He opened it and handed one to her. "Oh, Laurel. This is so messed up."

She took a tissue and dabbed at her eyes. "I told you I was a mess. Warned you that you didn't want to be involved with me."

"That's crazy talk. None of this is your fault."

"No, but I have issues because of it."

"Your issues don't scare me, Laurel. I'm just grateful to be here with you."

"Shit." She sniffed and wiped her cheeks with the backs of her fingers. "I swore I'd never cry over that bastard again."

"That's easy to say, but damn. A person doesn't go through that without some scars."

She expelled a tear-stained laugh. "Oh, don't I know it. I've battled my scars for years, and, goddamn it, I want to move on with my life."

Pieces clicked into place like tumblers in a lock. "With someone safe."

She grew very still. "Yes."

"And you don't believe that's me."

Her pause nearly killed him.

"I don't know. I didn't think so at first. You come across as a player, and I don't know what my heart can take. I sure as hell know that I don't want a setback and then another five, ten, fifteen years before I feel like I can breathe again. I know there are no guarantees in life and that looking for love can be an enormous risk for someone like me. I was hoping to mitigate the damages by picking someone who seemed safe."

She dropped her chin onto her knuckles and released a troubled sigh.

He ached to scoop her into his arms and hold her and kiss all her fears away. But he'd have to earn that right first. The only good part was that she was still here, sitting next to him on a log bench in the mountains. She had to trust him somewhat, or she wouldn't have let him near her.

Hope sparked inside him, and he clung to it like a lifeline. He'd dated plenty of other women and had probably earned the title she had given him. But he'd met no one like Laurel, and he knew without a doubt if he lost her, he'd never recover.

"What if we take it slow?" Slow was better than nothing, and if it meant he'd win her heart, he'd be a fucking snail. "We can be friends for a while first."

She snorted. "Friends? I can't be friends with a man who kisses me like you do."

"I see." She was asking him to back off.

"You don't see." She shifted on the log. "I like you, Charlie. I like the way I feel when I'm with you. You make me think there's hope for me after all."

Gratitude poured over him like a warm rain. "Of course there's hope for you." He just prayed there was hope for him as well.

She released a sigh, rattled by nerves. "But, like I said before, you scare the hell out of me."

He nodded, finally understanding. "Can I tell you something?"

She lifted her chin and met his gaze.

"You scare the hell out of me, too."

17

Laurel woke the next morning in a haze of warmth and happiness. She couldn't remember having as much fun as she had at Afton's wedding and then during her and Charlie's trek into the mountains. She could see herself falling for him, and she hadn't lied when she'd said he scared the hell out of her.

Rhythmic sounds of breathing floated into her consciousness, and she froze. Slowly, she lifted her head and gazed over her shoulder. Charlie lay only inches away, his expression relaxed in slumber.

Shit. He'd stayed the entire night. He hadn't wanted to leave her alone after their emotional evening, and he'd asked if he could hold her until she fell asleep. But it appeared he'd fallen asleep as well.

Carefully, she turned and sat up so she could fully see him. Jasper had joined them on the bed and lay curled against Charlie's other side. He whined softly, but didn't move.

Her heart ached at the endearing sight. The fact that she could picture this in her future did scare the hell out of her. The more she was around Charlie, the more she wondered if she could overlook his flirtatious ways. He'd sent Lexie away the previous night, hadn't he? She could see a person dating many while he waited to meet *the one*.

Could she be the one for him?

Charlie's eyes opened and locked on her, sending her insides into a frenzied dance of nerves and need. Jasper thumped his tail in delight now that Charlie was awake.

"Good morning." He sounded adorably sleepy, and she ached to run her fingers through his mussed hair.

"Morning." She'd changed the previous night into a t-shirt and flannel shorts, but he still wore his wedding clothes minus the jacket and shoes. "I thought you were only staying until I fell asleep."

A guilty grin curved his lips, the same lips who'd so expertly kissed her the previous night. "I didn't mean to stay all night." He scratched behind Jasper's ears, who promptly rolled over to have his tummy rubbed, too. "I'd planned on leaving, but you fell asleep on my arm and I didn't want to wake you. I thought I'd wait until you moved. I dozed, but every time I woke, you were still there."

She'd clung to him in her sleep? She focused on the happy German Shepherd pup now laying with his tongue lolling to the side to hide her embarrassment. "Sorry. I didn't realize."

He snorted. "I'm not sorry. I slept better than I have in ages."

What could she say to that? She had as well. "Um...breakfast?"

He lifted the pup to the side and sat. "I can't."

Her spirits plummeted. "Afraid I'll kill you with my cooking?" she asked in a teasing voice to hide her dismay.

"No, not even. But I need to be at the distillery early. I'm probably already late. I told Afton I'd manage affairs while she's on her honeymoon."

That's right. Afton was gone. How could she have forgotten? "No worries. Maybe another time." She acted as though he turned down a piece of gum instead of rejecting spending time with her.

"I accept. Does that include the sleepover beforehand?"

She snorted a laugh. "You wish."

"I do wish." He tugged her until she fell against him. He wrapped his arms tightly around her, and she worked hard to withhold an audible sigh of contentment. "In the meantime, can I cook dinner for you? Tonight? At six?"

"Tonight?" Her thoughts raced as ingrained fears jumped to the surface. Her immediate reaction was to say no. But she didn't want to be that woman anymore. "Yes. I'd love that. What will you be making?"

"A culinary surprise designed to steal your heart and soul so that you'll be mine forever."

"Oh, wow." She laughed. "Stop teasing me."

"Okay." He agreed with a laugh that rumbled through his chest and into her heart. He held her for a long moment before he kissed her head. "I don't want to go," he mumbled.

She didn't want him to leave, either. She wanted to stay like they were forever, intertwined in each other's arms, listening to his steady heartbeat. The safest place she knew.

That realization stunned her. She'd been so worried about letting him close, but right now, she felt untouchable.

"You'll be at my house at six?" he asked in a low voice.

"Yes." She pulled from him and caught his gaze.

He stared at her for a long, hard moment and then shook his head. "Today will drag like a beast, but I'd better get to it." He placed a quick kiss on her lips before he stood.

He checked his phone and then looked at her. "Ten hours."

She swallowed past her excitement and nodded.

"Why don't you bring your pup, too?" He tipped his head playfully at Jasper. "Max would love a friend."

————

A brilliant sun hovered in the west sky as Laurel made the short trek from her house to her Jeep, with Jasper in tow. She bent to lift the pup to put him in her vehicle and was surprised how much heavier he seemed than the last time when she'd taken him in for shots. "Wow, little buddy. You're packing on the pounds."

He barked, taking her words for praise. By the time he was fully grown, he'd weigh around ninety pounds. Big enough to defend her. She couldn't wait until he could start hiking with her.

In that moment, she realized Jasper had wormed his way into her heart, and she couldn't let him go.

When she reached the newest and only subdivision in Aspen where Charlie had built his home, her butterflies returned full force. She exhaled a deep breath and focused on relaxing her muscles. Surprisingly, the typical underlying nausea didn't accompany the fluttering this time.

"I think this might be okay, Jasper. You like Charlie, too, right?" She snuck a glance in his direction, but he was too busy sticking his nose out the window to answer. "Well, even if you don't say it, I know you do. You guys were all cuddled up in my bed this morning. Made me a little jealous."

Jasper still didn't look, and she rolled her eyes at her silly attempt at conversation.

She made a right turn and then a left one a few moments later before she spotted Charlie's truck parked in the drive of a new, brown-brick rambler at the end of the street. Half the lots in this section were claimed by houses, but the contractor had left many of the original pines and aspens so it didn't seem like a desolate area waiting for landscaping. Lush, freshly mown grass surrounded Charlie's house, though the flower beds had yet to be planted.

She shut off her engine and climbed out, calling Jasper to do the same. He ran toward the house and sniffed near the base of the stairs first, before climbing them to inspect two red Adirondack chairs that waited quietly on the porch.

Nervous energy sparked and popped inside her like a live wire. She smoothed the front of the lightweight periwinkle sweater she wore over a dark blue tank top. She'd hoped the addition dressed up her outfit enough that she didn't seem too casual. Even at work, Charlie usually wore nice clothes, and she didn't want to revert to the faded t-shirts and jeans she'd worn most of her life to warn off any potential suitors.

She lifted her hand to ring the doorbell, but before she could, Charlie swung open the door. Jasper dashed between his legs to greet Max. The black Border Collie sniffed his new friend as his tail wagged wildly. Then Max yipped and dashed toward her, as happy to see her as she was to see him. After allowing her to give him multiple kisses, he chose Jasper's company over hers.

She swiftly glanced at Charlie, surprised and pleased to find him in a faded Dodge t-shirt and ripped jeans. He'd tied a crisp white apron around his waist, and somehow that made him look hotter. "I think it's safe to say they like each other," she said.

"Definitely." He stepped back to let her enter and then shut the door behind her. "You look really nice. And I look like a slob. Give me a second to change."

"No." Without thinking, she grabbed his arm to stop him.

She swallowed, trying to calm her nerves. "I like comfortable clothes. Don't change on my account."

He pointed toward a hole near his midsection and sent her a sarcastic look. "This goes beyond comfortable. Don't you think?"

She shrugged out of her sweater, leaving her shoulders and arms bare, significantly lowering her dressed up look. "There. Now we match. If you want me to take off my shoes and go barefoot, I will."

He seared her with a heated gaze as he surveyed her in a slow, deliberate fashion. "I'll like you no matter what you wear or what you don't."

Heat rushed up her cheeks. She grappled for a comeback and came up empty.

He shut her mouth with the tip of one finger before he kissed her. "God, you're adorable. Come on into the kitchen. Dinner is about ready." He sauntered off as though he didn't have a care in the world.

She dropped her purse and sweater on a nearby chair and followed.

His home was gorgeous. Rich, dark woods with brown and gold accents welcomed her. The leather couch in his living room looked brand new, along with most of the other furnishings.

His kitchen was a masterpiece on its own. Brass-bottomed pots hung above a state-of-the-art gas stove. And the stainless-steel French door refrigerator put her little white one to shame. The opulent decor continued in this room and made her feel as though she'd entered a richly-appointed paradise. "I thought you were a starving chef opening his first restaurant."

He laughed. "If it wasn't for the money that I made in the corporate world before I escaped, I'd be on the streets."

The scents rising from whatever he had on the stove coaxed

a rumble from her stomach. She placed a hand over her belly, hoping he hadn't heard. "That smells incredible."

"Have a seat at the bar, and you can talk to me while I finish."

She climbed onto a comfortable, swiveling leather seat while he poured a glass of wine and then held it out to her. "Thank you."

She sniffed before taking a sip. "Very nice."

"Nothing but the best for you, darlin'."

She chuckled and shook her head at his flirty behavior. "Was that your plan? To ply me with delicious food and wine and cause me to lose my inhibitions?"

He added a pinch of something from a bowl and stirred. "Maybe?"

She couldn't imagine anything more attractive than watching this man with his killer green eyes and devastating smile cook for her. She was in big trouble indeed.

And she didn't care one bit.

She sipped her wine and watched with fascination as he created culinary art. When he finished, he plated up their dinners and headed for the table. "Grab my glass, will you?" he asked.

She leaned across the counter and wrapped her fingers around the stem. When she stood, the room tilted and then righted itself. Apparently, she'd had enough to grow tipsy. For a second, she was mortified, and then she decided she didn't care about that, either. If she drank too much and couldn't drive home, she'd crash at his house like he had at hers. She had Jasper with her, and she'd fed and played with the rest of the shelter animals before she left.

Charlie stood next to the table and outright stared as she approached. Seductive appreciation burned in his eyes and fanned the flames already charring her insides. She stopped next to him, held out his glass, and glanced up. "Thank you for cooking for me, Charlie."

He took the glass and set it on the table, never breaking their connected gazes as he did. Then he took her glass as well and set it aside. "You're welcome."

Her breaths grew deeper as she held his stare. He wrapped an arm around her waist, and she didn't protest when he pulled her against him. "Is this okay?"

She nodded and shivered as their bodies connected in all the right places. Slowly, he lowered his head, and her eyes fluttered shut when his lips claimed hers.

He took his time, drawing sweet kisses from her. She tasted the wine on his lips and sizzled from the heat emanating from his body. With her fear firmly locked away, she threaded her fingers through his soft hair and held him while he ravaged her with his mouth.

A half-sigh, half-moan escaped her when he pulled back. He stared into her eyes for a long time, and she searched his as well. He wasn't at all what she was looking for.

He was so much more.

Stronger, steadier, funnier, and a hell of a lot sexier than Riley. How could she have missed that about him in the first place?

Fear, her brain reminded her. Yes, she'd been afraid of feeling this much.

He drew a finger down the side of her cheek. "If we don't stop, I'll be having you for dinner."

She released a breathy laugh. "Would that be a problem?"

He closed his eyes for a long moment before meeting her gaze again. "Yes. You're not ready. Friends first, remember?" He slid a chair out from the table and held it for her.

She brushed against him and then sat. "I believe I argued that point already."

"Maybe so, but I'm not about to rush things and then scare you away." He took his seat, lifted a fork, and then pointed at the filled plate in front of her. "Dig in. I want to know what you think of my lemon asparagus salmon. If you like it, I think I'll add it to the menu."

18

"Oh, my God." Laurel leaned back in her chair and wrapped her hands across her belly. "I'm so full. I should have stopped a long time ago, but it was all so good."

Charlie grinned. "Always good to know when I've satisfied my lady."

Laurel snorted, but smiled.

He exhaled and slid back his chair. "Would the lady and her pup care to accompany me and my dog on a walk? It helps with digestion. Then later, I'll tempt you with dessert."

"Or maybe I'll tempt you."

He laughed as though she was kidding, but she wasn't so sure that she was.

An hour later, after exiting the subdivision and traversing a nearby trail that took them up into the hills, Laurel and Charlie neared his house again. He'd held her hand the entire time, and she'd loved every minute.

One thing was for sure. From day one, as long as they were on comfortable terms, she and Charlie had never struggled with conversation. Another thing she couldn't say about Riley.

Charlie let both dogs off their leashes to run in the backyard while they claimed another set of chairs outside his back door.

"I have to confess something," Charlie said.

He didn't seem upset by whatever it was, so she took his cue and kept her tone lighthearted. "And what would that be?"

"After the raving reviews I received from Afton's wedding reception, I did something really stupid. I invited my family to the restaurant. Told them it was to celebrate my grand opening and that I expected them all to be there."

She widened her eyes. He'd said his family didn't support him in his endeavor at all. "That was brave of you after your previous experience. Do you think they'll come?"

He paused for a moment. "I don't know, but I think they'd better."

As much as he grumbled about them, she sensed he still craved their approval. Especially from his father. "I hope they don't disappoint you."

He squeezed her hand and caught her gaze. "I'd like you to be there, too."

His invitation quickened her pulse. "Me? Why?"

He shrugged. "Moral support. Plus, I'd like them to meet you."

She laughed to stave off her anxiety. "Meeting the family already?"

"If you're not comfortable, I don't want to—"

"I'll be there, Charlie." She would, she realized, whenever he needed her.

"Thank you." He held out a hand. "Come here."

She inhaled a quick breath and stood. She kept her gaze on him as he took her hand and pulled her toward him. He didn't stop until she was sitting across his lap and he'd cradled her against him.

She sighed in response. This was it. Exactly where she wanted to be.

He tilted her face toward him. "I don't think I could ever tire of this."

"No?" she asked softly.

"No." He tilted his head to hers, giving her a sweet kiss.

She loved it, but she missed the passion of his first kiss. When he made to pull away, she slipped her arm from between them and slid it around his neck, erasing some of the distance between them.

He seemed to hold back, and she feared she knew why. He'd talked about taking things slowly. But there was a difference between that and not moving at all. She had thought she'd clarified that she was ready to leave the past behind and move on with her future. Despite her issues, she didn't want to be handled with kid gloves.

She wanted him to treat her like a woman, one that he desired. This was a new frontier for her, and she was ready to climb that mountain.

When he ended their kiss, she took a moment to catch her breath. But she wasn't finished. She needed more, and they had only just begun. She flattened her palm against his pecs and allowed the tips of her fingers to follow the curves. His shoulders were wide and strong, and she gripped one before she slid her hand down his bicep to his forearm.

She ran her fingertips over his forearm, allowing the hairs to glide past, before she stopped and dragged her nails back down to his wrist. She wanted to feel him, every part of him.

He maneuvered his hand until it covered hers, and he held it tight against his stomach. "You're going to drive me insane if you don't stop."

She wiggled her fingers as she held his gaze, gripping his t-shirt and pulling upward until she found bare skin. "What's wrong with insane?"

His laugh came out strangled. "I recognize now that you haven't had much experience with men—"

"You're the first guy I kissed."

"What?" he seemed more than a little surprised.

She slid her hand across his stomach, and he inhaled sharply. "Laurel, please. Know when you kiss and touch a guy like you are, you make it harder and harder for a man to stop."

The strength that lay beneath his soft skin thrilled her. "Does that mean that you're one of those men who thinks no means yes?" she teased.

"Of course not. What I mean is you're torturing the hell out of me. Guys like to fool around, but there comes a point when it's cruel to keep pushing him." He clamped his hand over hers once again.

She grinned. "Blue balls, I believe it's called?"

He stood up so fast she thought he might drop her, but she landed with her feet solidly on the ground. He touched the tip of her nose with his finger. "You are a tease. Come on, boys," he called to the dogs, and they both came running.

When they were all inside, Charlie strode to the sink and downed a large glass of water. Laurel walked up behind him, slid her hands around his waist, and laid her head on his back. "I'm sorry."

He turned and wrapped his arms around her before searching her eyes for several long moments. "It's okay. I'm just trying my best to do right by you."

His caring touched her deeply. "Do you remember when I told you I'm ready to claim my life?"

He nodded.

She exhaled a slow breath and slid her hand beneath his shirt again. "I'm not teasing you, Charlie."

He blinked and then stared as though he had a hard time comprehending her words. That was okay. She'd help him understand.

She placed both hands behind his neck and drew his face toward her. Then she kissed him with everything she had. She might not be an expert, but she mimicked how he'd kissed her before.

He groaned, and she took that as a sign she was doing just fine.

"Laurel," he whispered against her mouth, but he tightened his hold on her.

"Shhh..." She gripped the bottom of his t-shirt and drew it higher until she had it over his head. Her breath whooshed out at the sight of so much glorious skin and muscle. She'd seen naked men before, but none this close, and none that she could touch.

She pressed her nose to his bare skin and breathed in his pure, warm essence. Incredible. Then she tasted him and kissed her way over his collarbone to his neck.

"Holy mother," he hissed.

"I don't think she needs to be included in this," Laurel teased.

"God, I'd say not." He pulled away from her again. "Laurel, I'm not going to make love to you in the kitchen. If this is your first time—"

"It is."

He shook his head, bewilderment etched on his face. "We're going to do this right."

A shiver strong enough to rock the valley rolled through her. *Damn.*

"Come with me." He held out his hand, and she gladly took it.

She followed him up the stairs and into his bedroom, where he shut the door to keep out the dogs. He didn't waste a second afterward. He claimed her with fierce kisses, pushing her until her back was against the door and he'd pinned her with his hard body.

Blood swirled in her head until nothing existed except for her and Charlie. Sensations replaced thoughts. Need replaced fear. He owned her heart and soul.

After a powerfully sensuous kiss, she gasped for air.

He dropped his head to her shoulder and breathed deeply. "I'm so fucking turned on that I'm afraid I'll lose control and hurt you," he said between breaths. "Tell me if I do."

She lifted his head and met his gaze. "You're not going to hurt me. I want this. With all my heart."

He nodded and his gaze dropped lower to her tank top. He drew his hands over her shoulders and down, gently caressing her. "Your skin is incredible."

She exhaled as everything in her melted and pooled at her core. "Your touch is incredible."

He smiled. With his gaze pinned to hers, he slipped her top over her head. A rush of air and the look on his face narrowed her nipples to sharp, aching points. She needed him to touch her.

"Black bra, huh?" he said, with a trace of humor in his voice. "For some reason, I expected white."

She snorted softly. "I might be inexperienced, but trust me, I'm not a nun."

He arched a brow. "So, you've..."

Heat flooded her cheeks, and she rolled her eyes. "You don't live to be my age and not learn a little about your body. At least most people don't."

"Hmm..." Approval flickered in his eyes. "I have a feeling you're going to learn a lot more today."

A deep yearning tightened her core. "Maybe so," she said breathlessly.

Slowly, he slid a strap from her shoulder and placed his lips where it had been. She closed her eyes on a shuddering sigh. He did the same with the other side, and she could barely breathe.

He stared at her as he traced a curving, sensuous trail across her collarbone, down between her breasts. With excruciating slowness, he drew his thumbs across her nipples. "Nice," he whispered. Then he moved his hands to her back, where he unhooked her bra and freed her breasts from their constraints.

His eyes widened as he exposed her to him. "Ah, fuck. I'm the luckiest man in the world."

She tried to laugh, but it came out as a breathy whoosh instead.

"Remember, you'll tell me if I hurt you, right?" He said it as though it was her last chance to decide between safe or the experience of a lifetime.

She nodded.

He cupped her again and lowered his head. When his mouth claimed her nipple, she thought she'd die from pleasure. Sensations coursed through her, heading straight for her nether region. Her body grew soft, and she clung to him to keep from falling.

Instinctively, she arched her back and tipped her chin upward. She couldn't move, couldn't respond. She could only take the glorious gift he offered her. He kissed his way to her other breast and plied his sweet assault there as well.

When he made his way to her neck and then crushed her against him, she was sure she'd never think straight again.

He lifted her and carried her to the bed, where he stripped her jeans from her. He removed his, along with his boxer briefs.

She stared at the sight of his member standing thick and proud. She'd always feared she'd be afraid to be with a man, for them to be naked together, but all she experienced was hot, aching lust.

He crawled toward her from the bottom of the bed, looking every inch a predator. She inhaled and widened her eyes. He grinned in response.

"Oh, damn," she whispered.

"That's right," he said, his voice low and sexy.

When he reached her thighs, he laid next to her and propped himself up on one elbow. With his free hand, he traced lazy circles, winding his way toward the spot she most wanted him to touch.

He took too long. "Charlie," she begged in a breathless whisper.

He focused his heated gaze on her, and she was happy to see he was as affected as she was by their play. "What?" he asked softly.

"Touch me."

A wicked grin crossed his lips. "Oh, I'm planning to, darlin'." He touched the most sensitive part of her, and she gasped. She still wore her panties, but the feel of him there was so intimate, so incredibly delicious, that she couldn't help herself.

His breaths came deeper as he slipped a finger beneath her panties and found his way to her core.

"Holy mother," he said again, but she couldn't respond. Her eyes rolled back in her head as her breathing momentarily stopped. She spread her legs wider and gripped the quilt.

"These definitely have to go." He dispensed with her panties in record time, but instead of sliding his finger into her again, he dipped his head between her legs. She opened her mouth to protest, but the feel of his tongue stole everything. She bucked as a blinding spasm ripped through her.

He continued torturing her with pleasure until she settled,

and then he laughed. "Oh, darlin'. Did I mention I'm the luckiest man?"

She tried to moisten her lips, but her mouth had gone bone dry. "What did you do to me?"

He crawled up next to her and tucked a thigh between hers. The hard length of him pressed against her, promising her they were far from finished. Every inch of her was alive with buzzing excitement as he stared into her eyes. "You never...on your own?"

"Not like that." Nothing like that. She'd had quivers that she'd assumed were orgasms, but nothing mind-blowing like what he'd made her feel.

He traced a slow circle around her nipple, and it puckered in anticipation. "Would you like another?"

"Another?" she asked breathlessly. *"Yes."*

He drew her nipple deep into his mouth, sucking and nipping until everything tightened into an exquisite ball of powerful energy. Then he moved on top of her.

She sank into the bed from his weight, and her world became solely focused on the hard length of him pushing against her. He captured her mouth and plied her with heated kisses.

Then he was at her core.

He moved inside with one powerful thrust, and she gasped, her eyes flying wide. "I'm sorry," he whispered against her hair as he pulled out and slowly entered again.

The brief flash of pain dissolved into heated, lovely friction. She drew in a breath and lost her thoughts in the sensations of him moving, claiming her with each thrust, and the way her body accepted him.

With pleasure once again thrumming through her veins, she wrapped her legs around him and joined him by rocking her pelvis to receive his thrusts. The sound of his groan increased the tension building inside her exponentially. He pumped into her two more times before she exploded into another wave of delirium.

She clung to him and panted to catch her breath and her bearings.

"You're incredible, Laurel," he whispered against her ear, and his thrusting gained in power and intensity. She held tight as he sought his pleasure, and then he stiffened and groaned again before he collapsed on top of her.

He rolled to the side, both of them panting, and she tried to wrap her mind around what had just happened. Her experience seemed unworldly, and she wasn't sure she could describe it in so many words.

She willingly moved into his arms as he gathered her to him. He kissed her head and held her tight.

"Thank you for that," he said, his voice still breathless. "I didn't hurt you, did I?"

"No." The quick flash of pain was long in the past. "You were amazing. I feel amazing."

His chuckle rumbled against her ear. "Same."

Long moments passed in a haze of pleasure and silence. He caressed her arm and then squeezed her tightly against him. "You're staying the night, right?"

"I need to go home and take care of the animals, but I'll come back," she whispered without hesitating. She couldn't walk away from this if her life depended on it.

"Good. I'll come with you."

19

Charlie constantly glanced at the clock in Sagecreek's kitchen while he prepped for that evening's dinner menu.

His assistant lifted her jaw and caught Charlie's attention. Short and slight in stature, Nicole Walker didn't look older than fourteen, but her expression earned her every one of her twenty-four years. "You've looked at that clock ten times in the past minute."

"I know." Dammit. "My family's scheduled to arrive at six-thirty, but they'll more than likely show up early." His father was never late for anything.

Nicole rolled her eyes. "I don't know why you picked our busiest time to host them. Wouldn't it be less stressful to have them earlier or later, or on another day?"

He whisked the raspberry vinaigrette that he'd serve with the salad. "I'm sure, but I wanted them all to see the restaurant thriving and not looking like a ghost town, doomed to failure." And he wanted them to love Laurel.

She chuckled. "I guess so. Still seems crazy to me."

He glanced at the clock again. Five-thirty. He'd guess they'd arrive about six, so that gave him only fifteen minutes to get everything in order. He'd asked Laurel to show before then, but she hadn't appeared yet, adding more stress.

He honestly didn't care if they approved of her or not. She was the missing piece in his life, and he wouldn't let her go for anything. But life would certainly be easier if they blended well. He'd left his family in pursuit of his dreams, but he'd never be able to sever the connection completely. Nor did he want to.

Unless they didn't accept Laurel.

The double-hinged door swung open, and he jerked his gaze upward. *Laurel.* He didn't care if she wore jeans and a t-shirt or the stunning black cocktail dress she did now. She would forever be the most beautiful woman in the world to him.

He wiped his hands on a towel and strode toward her.

Her dress was simple in its perfection, emphasizing her lovely curves perfectly. Auburn hair hung in loose, sexy curls, and red lipstick drew his attention to the engaging smile he yearned to see every day. "My God, you're beautiful."

Happiness beamed on her face, and he was grateful he was the man who'd put it there. "Stop. You're going to make me blush."

He cupped her face and smiled. "I love it when you blush," he whispered in her ear. He gave her the softest of kisses, not wanting to mess up those succulent red lips. He'd save that for later.

She pulled away and fanned her face with her hand. "I'm already beyond nervous. Don't make it worse."

Damn, she was cute. "Don't be nervous. They're just regular people."

"No, they're not. They're your family, and—and corporate, stuffy people who are hard to impress." She held up her hand when he started to speak. "Don't deny it. You're the one who told me about them."

He pulled her close again until her hips snuggled up against his. "Yes, I said that because they'd pissed me off with their narrow-minded attitudes. But don't forget that we grew up in the same house together, so my brothers are probably more like me than you realize."

"It's your father who scares me the most, anyway."

He snorted. "Yeah, he can be a tough bastard, but he agreed to come tonight, right? Maybe he only wants to see if I'll fail. But I hope he'll be proud of me."

She stared into his eyes, heating his body. "You're amazing. Do you know that? Few would leave a secure future to follow their dreams. I really admire you for that."

"That's because you're as addicted to adventure as I am."

She laughed. "Almost."

His newest server, a young, blond woman named Leisa, popped her head into the kitchen. "Your family is here, Charlie."

Her words caught him like an uppercut punch, and he emptied his lungs in a quick rush. "Great. Seat them out on the courtyard near the back, where they'll have the best view of the hills. Then take them the fried brie and the bottle of Riesling I selected earlier. Tell them I'll be out shortly. I just need to put the finishing touches on this and turn the kitchen over to Nicole."

"Are you sure?" his assistant asked with a heavy dose of sarcasm. "It might kill you if you do."

"Shut up, Walker, and get to work."

Charlie held Laurel's gaze until Leisa walked away. "Do you want to go with her? I'll be out soon."

Laurel widened her eyes into ovals. "You want to send me into the wolves' den alone? No way."

"Dude," Nicole chided.

Charlie held up a hand. "Stop. Both of you. This is nothing but a quaint family gathering. Nothing that should get your panties into a bunch."

Laurel snickered, and Charlie caught the conspiratorial look she aimed at Nicole. "Too late, Charlie. You can't change our minds about them now. I'll wait for you."

Charlie gave specific instructions to Walker on how to finish their main dish, noting that she should send out the spinach pear salads in ten minutes. "Showtime."

"You'll be great," Laurel whispered. "Don't worry. I'll be there to make sure they don't eat you."

He snorted. God, he loved this woman.

A soft summer breeze greeted them as he and Laurel entered the courtyard, and Charlie couldn't have asked for a more perfect evening. All eyes turned to them as they approached. Immediately, he was reminded he was the baby in the family. The spoiled one. The unappreciative one.

Would he ever live that down?

His father sat at the head of the table, of course. He never let an opportunity for a power play slide. His silver hair matched the gray in his dinner jacket. The lavender shirt and purple tie he wore complimented it well. They all knew his father had his assistant to thank for that.

His oldest brother, Samuel, had claimed one side with his cosmopolitan chic fiancée, Frances, at his side. Kenneth, brother number two, sat opposite his father. Damn if they didn't both look like younger versions of their father, except for Kenneth's goatee. Soon they'd have the wrinkles and heart conditions as well if they weren't careful.

Charlie stuck out a hand to shake. "Dad."

His father stood and returned the gesture. "Good to see you, Charles."

"I'd like to introduce Laurel Ewing. I've asked her to join us this evening. Laurel, this is my father, Donald Blackmore."

Both brothers lifted intrigued brows, and Frances's mouth curved into a sly smile as Laurel shook Donald's hand. Charlie continued the introductions until his family had all exchanged pleasant greetings with Laurel, and he prayed the rest of the evening would go just as well.

Charlie didn't miss the quick look of fear in Laurel's face as he pulled out the chair next to his father for her. He would have warned her of his ploy to tame the lion by placing a beautiful woman next to him, but Laurel would have fretted about it for days in advance.

She'd be fine. His father would spend considerable time trying to charm her, taking the heat off him, and she'd have a great evening despite his covert maneuvers.

His family kept the conversation lighthearted and polite through most of the meal, and Laurel seemed to relax. The beef fillet with Irish whiskey and cream pan sauce was perfect, and everyone, including his dad, seemed to enjoy it. Leisa would deliver dessert, the final blow, in just a few moments.

Samuel turned to Laurel. "Charlie said you're a writer. That you've even published an article in Reader's Digest."

An adorable blush colored Laurel's cheeks as she shot him a look that said he'd pay later. "Oh, well. I'm mostly picked up by smaller magazines and newspapers."

Charlie grinned. Beautiful, talented, and his. At least for tonight. "She writes articles targeted toward adventurers."

Donald straightened in his seat, obviously interested. "Is that so? Like what?"

Laurel shrugged. "Climbing, high-country backpacking, rafting. Outdoorsy stuff."

"With a little danger thrown in," Charlie added, wanting to impress them all with his choice of women as well.

"Ever biked down the slopes at Sundance ski resort?" Kenneth asked.

Laurel shook her head. "No, but I've wanted to forever."

"It's amazing," Samuel added. "Fast-paced thrills through incredible scenery. Are you good on a bike?"

"I haven't done any trail riding since last summer, and definitely nothing downhill like that, but it sounds right up my alley. It would make a great article for local folks."

Frances leaned forward. "I'd say you're in luck. Kenneth knows that area well, and I bet he'd take you."

"Really? I would love that." Funny how a little talk about Laurel's favorite subject, and she suddenly seemed completely in her element.

Kenneth nodded, seeming more than willing, which warmed Charlie's heart. Maybe Laurel and his family would mesh after all. "Sure. I haven't been this summer, either, and I'd love to go. How about this Friday? We could make a day of it. I'm sure you'll want to ride down the mountain more than once. I have a connection with some people there. I bet if I told them you were doing an article, they'd comp some, if not all, of the lift rides to the top."

"That would be..." Laurel's expression fell, taking him with her. "My mom works a double shift on Fridays." She turned to Charlie. "Afton's out of town, and I can't leave the shelter that long."

"Shelter?" Frances asked.

"She lives at a small farm that she and my business partner have turned into a local pet shelter." He took Laurel's hand. "I'd be happy to watch them so you can go. Except not this Friday. I have a business meeting in Salt Lake. Tying up some loose ends. Any day next week and I'm at your complete disposal."

He would have promised her the world for the smile she gave him in return.

"That would be so fantastic." Laurel glanced around the table, her expression glowing. "This is so exciting."

"Most likely, you'll be gone most of the day," Samuel warned. "You'd better plan on staying overnight. Not good to drive the canyons in the dark, especially alone. We have a spare bedroom, if you don't mind staying with us."

"That would be perfect," Frances said. "We can have our turn with her and take her to dinner that night."

Leisa interrupted their conversation when she arrived with the bourbon pecan pie. Interest lit the faces of his family, and he held his breath, waiting for their reactions.

"Oh, my God, Charlie," Frances said around a mouthful. "This is incredible."

Samuel agreed.

Kenneth lifted his glass of wine. "Looks like you did well, little brother."

"I'd say," Frances offered.

Donald raised his glass. "It seems so, but don't forget, looks can be deceiving."

Disappointment fell over Charlie like a rain-soaked wool coat, and he set his drink down a little harder than he'd meant to. "Dammit, Dad. Can you not have a little faith in me, even just once?"

He'd finally said what he'd been thinking for years. He didn't know if it was because he'd been away from his father's influence for long enough, or if perhaps Laurel's support helped, but he was tired of ignoring the passive jabs.

His father choked on his sip of wine. "Excuse me?" He seemed genuinely shocked.

Laurel caught his hand beneath the table and squeezed.

Charlie exhaled a breath full of frustration. "Look at this place. It's gorgeous, and I'm damned proud of what I've built. You're the one who taught me about hard work and smart thinking. Just because I've applied it to a different area in life doesn't negate its value. Why can't you be proud, too?"

No one spoke while his father loosened his tie and then cleared his throat. "I'm sorry, Charles, but you'll never make here what you could have by working for me."

"It's not always about money, Dad. Sometimes, it's about happiness. I love what I do here. It doesn't feel like work, and I don't care if I drive a Maserati."

Frances looked at Samuel as though she was worried that he might agree and she'd have to give up her opulent lifestyle. God, love her.

Donald stared at him for a long moment. Charlie knew that look. It was the same one that appeared every time his father deliberated over a decision. "Well, I guess if you're happy."

His father had said the words he'd longed to hear, but Charlie was sure he still didn't truly understand. Maybe never would. But as long as he respected his decisions. "I am happy, Dad. I can't remember ever being happier."

"That's what's important," Laurel added, and Charlie knew then and there she was the woman for him. Even better, she seemed to like his family just fine. He'd worried for nothing.

When everyone had finally headed home and the restaurant was quiet, he and Laurel locked up the building and headed out the courtyard doors. He stopped her beneath the soft moonlight and pulled her into his arms. He had something in his heart that he could contain no longer.

She laughed as he danced with her to unheard music. "What are you doing?"

"This has been the most perfect night. Thanks to you."

She shook her head, but he could see he'd pleased her.

He drew a finger down her cheek. "Despite that, I think I'm in trouble."

She widened her eyes in concern. "Why?"

The slightest bit of guilt pinched him for teasing her. "I've done something I never thought I would."

She stopped dancing. "I'm sure it can't be that bad."

"Oh, but it is. You see, I've fallen for you, Laurel."

Her mouth formed into an O, and she blinked several times. "You have?" she asked softly. "Fallen?"

He tipped her chin up and stared into the most beautiful eyes he'd ever seen. "Fallen hard."

"Oh..."

He captured her lips with a kiss meant to steal her heart and destroy thoughts of any other men forever.

20

Laurel gazed out over the spread of thick pines at the Sundance ski resort as she adjusted the helmet on her head. She stood at the top of a mountain, surrounded by spectacular scenery, and all she could think about was Charlie stating he'd fallen for her.

Did that mean love? She thought maybe, but he hadn't used the word. She hadn't either. He'd caught her completely off guard with his announcement. Then he'd kissed her senseless before he took her home, and they'd made passionate love.

She'd never found the right opportunity to return his sentiment, and honestly, she wasn't sure what she'd say. He didn't seem disturbed by her lack of a declaration, so maybe he intended to give her time.

Did she love him? What was love, anyway?

Did she yearn to be with him every second he was away? Yes. Did she constantly consider what their life would be like together? Yes. Was his happiness the most important thing to her...

Yes.

Maybe she did love him.

She exhaled and refocused on the miles of evergreens spread out beneath her like a lush green carpet. They contrasted perfectly with the brilliant blue sky. Fresh, if somewhat thinner, air filtered through her lungs and she breathed deeper. "Magnificent view," she said to Kenneth.

Kenneth slipped on riding gloves. "Take it all in now because once we're on the trail, you'll be lost in the trees and moving fast."

She shifted her gaze to the dirt trail with a sharp decline that disappeared into the aspens and pines. "I can't say that doesn't intimidate the hell out of me."

He chuckled. "That's the whole point. Not much of an adrenaline rush if it doesn't. If you weren't an experienced biker, I might worry, but I think you'll love it. Just keep your eyes on the trail ahead to avoid hazards, and you'll be fine."

She smiled and nodded. Yes. The addictive rush. The one thing that had always ensured her that she was alive. Unlike those other girls.

When they were geared up, they moved toward the head of the trail. "You go first this time and show me the way, okay?" she asked.

"Sure thing. Holler if you need to stop, and I'll try to keep my eye on you as much as possible. Charlie would kill me if I let his lady get hurt." He winked, and she shook her head in embarrassment.

"Okay." Part of her wanted to argue that she wasn't his lady, but after Charlie's declaration the other night, she wondered if she just might be. She'd never had a boyfriend, and the whole thing felt wonderful and scary at the same time. Sort of like riding down a mountainside at full speed.

Kenneth mounted his bike and started their descent.

He rode fast.

But, God, it was exhilarating. Luckily, the trail was wide and grassy, and Laurel did her best to keep up. Her body jostled as she bounced over the uneven, rutted terrain that would be a ski trail in the winter. The afternoon sun shone brightly, leaving her warm beneath her biking gear.

Air whooshed around her as she followed Kenneth over the dusty, winding trails. Occasionally, he'd take a side excursion up and over a steeper part of the hillside, giving her an extra thrill.

Kenneth slowed as they entered the trees, and the trail grew much narrower. Dappled shade took over, giving her a respite from the sun, but she also had to keep her focus solely on the trail to avoid hazards. A branch grabbed for her sleeve as she overshot a turn, but she quickly righted herself.

Kenneth picked up speed, and she hurried to catch up. She did just as they burst from the trees out onto a wider trail again. They rode that way a bit more, and then they were back into the trees. The wooden jump near the end was a fun surprise, and far too soon, she found herself at the bottom of the mountain.

She pulled off her helmet, laughing. "Good God, that was awesome."

He grinned. "Told ya."

"Can we do it again?" And again.

Each time down the mountain grew easier. The dirt trail was more familiar, and she could glance away for seconds to appreciate the scenery when the path wasn't as treacherous. This made trip five for her, and she'd convinced Kenneth to let her go first.

Adrenaline rushed through her even faster without having him as a distraction. It was her, the bike, and nature. Nothing else existed in that moment. She lived for this, and she couldn't wait to share it with Charlie.

Halfway down, movement in the trees snatched her attention, and she inhaled in wonder at the sight of the magnificent buck grazing there. He lifted his majestic head, his rack regal and confident, and he didn't seem fazed by their presence in the least.

Just as she glanced back, she saw the rock, and her tire jerked as she struck it. Without warning, the bike tossed her from the seat. She hit the ground with a solid thud that ripped the oxygen from her lungs.

Dirt puffed around and everything went quiet. She tried to draw in a breath and panicked when she couldn't get enough air.

Kenneth skidded to a stop and dropped his bike beside her. "Oh, fuck. Are you okay?"

"I think so. Just—" She tried another breath.

"Just relax. Don't move until we're sure you haven't broken anything."

She mentally scanned her body for pain. "I'm okay. Knocked the wind. Out of me." She rolled to one elbow to test her movement.

He shook his head in admonition as he released a worried snort. "Don't do shit like that. You must pay attention."

"A deer. Distracted me." She inhaled a full breath and blew it out. Damn. She'd taken some spills during her adventures, but it never ceased to amaze her how quickly she could go from awesome to flat on her back in an instant. She lifted a hand and held it out to Kenneth.

"If you're sure..."

She nodded and then groaned as he helped her to a sitting position. Her head spun for a second and then cleared. She shrugged her shoulders and swiveled her head. Everything seemed to work fine. Thank God she'd worn a helmet, or her circumstances might be worse.

With Kenneth's help, she slowly got to her feet and then

glanced into his worried eyes. "I'm good. No doubt, I'll feel it tomorrow, but I think I'm ready to go."

He narrowed his gaze in uncertainty. "I don't know..."

"Really?" she countered. "What are you going to do? Call for Life Flight? They'd laugh you off this mountain. This isn't my first tumble. I'll be fine." Her humiliation was bad enough without him fussing over her.

He checked her bike for damage before he returned it to her. "Looks like it's okay, too. Have it checked by a professional when you get home to make sure you didn't bend the frame."

"I will." After she came up with a good enough story that wouldn't make her look like an imbecile.

Kenneth regarded her with a wary gaze. "Are you going to tell Charlie?"

She snorted. "Uh, no. Are you going to give me up?" One person knowing her shame was enough.

He grinned. "I think we have a pact."

"I'd say we do. We should probably get going. I'm going to need to shower before dinner."

He laughed and then climbed on his bike, and they took off down the hillside once again, this time at a much slower pace. Each pedal hurt her knee, but she ignored the pain and pushed on.

She liked Charlie's brother. Fun and crazy, handsome as well. It seemed to run in his family. And she liked that he seemed to enjoy her company, too. She looked forward to spending more time with him and Charlie on wild family adventures.

———

Laurel grimaced as she followed Frances into Salt Lake City's newest Greek restaurant, while Samuel held the door for them.

Even though she'd opted for flats instead of the high heels she'd brought specifically for dinner, her back muscles screamed in protest. She should be lying down with ice packs, but if she canceled dinner, she'd have to explain why. The last thing she wanted was to embarrass herself further with Charlie's family.

Frances had dressed in a smart cream silk shirt and short black skirt. Samuel wore a dinner jacket but had passed on a tie. They looked like the perfect cosmopolitan couple, and Laurel silently commended herself for borrowing a blue dress from Afton's closet. She'd been able to hide the bruising on her knee with a little makeup. If someone looked closely, she'd be busted, but otherwise she looked presentable.

The hostess sat them in a quiet corner that looked out onto the quaint east side street. Giant oaks grew along the parking strip, and from her vantage point, she could see the small fountain out front. If she hadn't been in so much pain, she would have thoroughly enjoyed the view.

"One of Charlie's old girlfriends, Siobhan, actually owns this place," Frances offered as she glanced over the menu.

Laurel jerked her gaze upward and then did her best to cover her reaction. "Is that so?"

"He's the one who recommended it to us. This will be our second time coming here in a week. Fantastic food." Frances looked pointedly at Samuel over the top of her menu. "They went to culinary school together, right?"

"Mm-hmm." He didn't bother to look up. "Worked together for a while, too, I believe."

"They've remained good friends since," Frances added and then laughed. "Donald actually liked her."

Samuel glanced at them both then. "Only because he was friends with her father."

Past girlfriends were not exactly a preferred subject for her. "It seems like a very nice place."

"It is," they both agreed, and then Frances quickly looked up. "Not that Donald didn't like you. He didn't say one bad thing on the way home after visiting Aspen, so I think he approves of your relationship with Charlie. Honestly, it took me a solid six months of dating Samuel before he'd give me the time of day."

Laurel smiled awkwardly, clueless as to an appropriate response. Her anxiety grew with each passing moment. Kenneth had been a delight, but Frances and Samuel seemed well out of her league.

Thankfully, she kept her composure throughout the meal. Her hosts were gracious enough, but she'd struggled to find common interests. Samuel wasn't as athletic as Kenneth, and Frances seemed fairly focused on shoe styles and her job as a junior partner at her legal firm.

Unfortunately, Laurel couldn't complain about the food. The faceless Siobhan could hands-down decimate any of her competition. Though Laurel hadn't cared about learning to cook in the past, she suddenly wished she could impress Charlie with her skills.

As she pondered ways to sneak ice into her room after they returned home without Samuel and Frances knowing, a lovely woman near her age approached. She'd piled messy auburn hair on top of her head in a sexy way that Laurel was sure she could never master. As her engaging green eyes focused on Laurel, she knew without a doubt the woman was Charlie's ex-girlfriend.

"Hey, guys." Even her smile was beautiful. "So good to see you again. Charlie said he was going to coerce you into coming, but I didn't expect to see you so soon, and you brought a friend."

"He actually convinced us to come last Sunday, too," Frances responded. "Your food was so good that we wanted to come back."

Siobhan laughed. "I swear that man could charm the pants off a nun, and he probably has."

Laurel swallowed as a thick band of anxiety wrapped around her neck.

"We didn't want to bother you," Frances continued. "I'm certain you stay plenty busy with your new place."

"Yeah." Siobhan looked around the room with a proud smile gracing her red lips. "It's my dream come true. I truly appreciate your support. I'll have to thank Charlie when I see him again."

See him again? Charlie had never mentioned Siobhan to her. Was she someone who was still important in his life?

Siobhan gave them all an exaggerated, guilty look. "I promised to try his new place, too, but I haven't made my way in that direction yet. I hope he'll forgive me."

"I'm sure he will," Samuel answered.

Frances released a small gasp. "Where are my manners? Siobhan, this is Laurel, Charlie's latest."

Charlie's latest? Her insides chilled as the blood drained to her feet.

"Laurel, please meet Siobhan. Salt Lake's newest restaurateur extraordinaire."

Siobhan's smile grew larger, and she stuck out a hand. Laurel begrudgingly shook it, working to keep an authentic smile on her face. "I'm pleased to meet you."

"Same," Siobhan said and pulled a chair from an empty nearby table. "I'll just sit for a minute. I've heard about you and your impressive writing skills."

Charlie had talked to this woman about her? Someone she'd never met? "Oh, really?"

"He gushed on and on last weekend while he was here."

Laurel took a sip of wine to force open her closed throat. "He did?"

"In fact, I should show you a photo we took. It's one of my favorites. I'm glad you're all here to see it." She slipped her phone from her slacks and tapped the screen a few times before she held it out. "Here."

Laurel glanced at the screen, and it might as well have ripped her heart straight from her chest. The photo was of Siobhan and Charlie with their faces close together, both smiling and holding glasses of wine, looking as though they couldn't be happier.

She pushed it away. "That's a very nice picture." She feared she'd throw up right in the center of the table.

Siobhan didn't seem fazed by her lack of enthusiasm. "We both promised we'd celebrate when we opened our own restaurants. We worked hard, and look at us now."

Us? She couldn't bear to listen to another word.

Samuel glanced at the picture. "Congratulations, Siobhan. You've both done well."

"We have, haven't we? I probably shouldn't gloat too much, but dammit, it feels good. Hey, how about dessert, on the house? Whatever you'd like."

"Oooh," Frances said with a smile.

If she had to stay one more minute, she'd likely die. "Would you mind if we get it to go? I'm not feeling so well."

Siobhan turned to her with a concerned look. "Not the food, I hope."

She inhaled a slow breath. "Just a long day."

"Kenneth had her out on the hills at Sundance. They rode most of the afternoon."

"Ah." Siobhan smiled as though that all made sense to her. "I went there with Charlie a while back. Not to ride bikes, but just to take in the amazing views from the ski lift."

———

Laurel wept silent tears as she sat holed up in Frances and Samuel's guest bedroom. Anxiety gripped her as she waited for the house to grow quiet, signaling the others had gone to bed. She clutched a pillow to her chest and held on to it as though it was her only lifeline at that moment.

Charlie's latest? Did none of them realize what an insult that was? Or were they so used to one woman in his life after another that they no longer cared?

She dropped her hands into her face as she replayed Siobhan's excitement of having Charlie celebrate opening night with her. She'd made it sound as though they were still very close, which obviously they were if Charlie had gone to her grand opening.

Laurel could only think of one reason Charlie would have hidden that from her.

Because he had something to hide. If Siobhan was only a friend, he would have mentioned her. It was an incredible coincidence that he and his ex-girlfriend would open restaurants within a week of each other. That was conversation worthy. He would have told her.

Unless he had something to hide.

Siobhan didn't seem worried about Laurel, but maybe she was one of those women who didn't mind multiple partners.

She wished she could convince herself she was jumping to a boatload of conclusions, but facts were facts. He'd been here the previous weekend celebrating with his ex-lover, and he hadn't mentioned a word to her. Not one word.

"Shit," she hissed. She should have listened to her intuition all those weeks ago. Her gut had told her to run. But, no. Her stupid heart laid itself bare for Charlie to slay at will.

Her counselor had warned her to take care, reminding her she hadn't had the experience with men like most women her age, which left her more susceptible. But she'd grown stronger, more confident.

She'd thought she was ready.

Maybe she wasn't cut out for romance, period. Some people weren't. Maybe her childhood experiences had damaged her trust forever. She'd done great in other areas of her life, and she was proud of it. She should have kept her focus there.

Dammit. She never would have looked twice at him, except for Afton's glowing recommendation. How could Afton have been so wrong?

Except...Charlie was a good man...or at least a good business partner. Afton was only looking at him from that perspective, and she'd been wrong.

So incredibly wrong.

God help her.

She needed to go home. Now. She couldn't face Frances or Samuel in the morning. Her eyelids would stay swollen for hours the next day. They'd know she'd been crying, and they'd want to know why.

Her throat constricted, and she squeezed her eyes shut as a fresh wave of pain steamrolled her. She clutched the pillow to her face as she tried to bury the sound of her crying while she waited until she could leave without notice.

21

A solid pounding reached through Laurel's haze of sleep and jerked her awake. Early morning sun streamed through her bedroom window, and for a moment, she had to remind herself she was home, safe in her own bed. Events of the previous evening rushed in like a freight train, and she considered that the pounding might have been only her aching head. Until another round ensued.

Damn. The rattling of the home's old wooden door speared her with a sense of panic, and she threw off her bed covers. In answer to her quick actions, her body screamed in protest, viciously reminding her of the tumble she'd taken on the mountain the previous day.

She made it halfway to the living room before her thoughts clicked into place and she realized who would be on the other side of her front door. She didn't want to face Charlie. Not now. Maybe not ever.

She needed time to gather her strength and formulate what she'd say. He'd fight her, she knew. After all, he didn't have a problem with the way things were.

She peeked out the front window to be sure who was on the other side. Quick, fierce pain rushed into her heart and left her shaking.

With her hand on the doorknob, she closed her eyes for a moment and blew out a breath. *She could do this.*

She pulled open the door and met Charlie's frantic gaze. He tugged her into his arms before she could stop him. "Thank God. When Samuel called to let me know you'd driven home last night, I tried your phone. When you didn't answer, I thought the worst."

Fresh waves of despair threatened to drag her under. She summoned the frigid lack of emotion she'd used many times over the years, self-preservation at its finest, and she pulled back. "I turned my phone off."

"Why?" He stopped short and widened his eyes. "Oh, my God. Laurel. What's wrong? Samuel said you hadn't felt well during dinner. But you've been crying."

That he'd noticed only made things worse.

Did the man think she was an idiot? Of course, Samuel might not have imparted that they'd visited Siobhan's restaurant last night. At this moment, Charlie probably didn't have a clue about what she'd discovered. Or maybe he did, but didn't think it was any big deal.

"This isn't going to work, Charlie." Her voice came out calm, flat.

He drew his eyebrows down. "What isn't?"

She sensed the moment when he figured it out.

"*Us?* You mean us?"

There was that *us* word again. "If I recall correctly, Siobhan used that word last night when she spoke of you and her at her celebration party the previous weekend. I assume that was the supposed *business meeting* you needed to attend."

Color drained from Charlie's face, and he looked as sickly as she felt. "No."

"Yes," she argued. "I'm sure you never thought I'd meet Siobhan in a million years, or that I'd discovered what you really did last weekend, but I did."

He shook his head. "No. You've got this all wrong."

"Really?" She stared hard into his eyes, the same eyes that had once made her feel so loved. And she'd trusted. Oh, God. How she'd trusted. "So, you weren't with her last weekend?"

Even if he tried, he couldn't lie his way out of this one.

"Yes, I was there, but it's not what you think."

"What I thought was that you were in Salt Lake for a business meeting, not to schmooze with your old girlfriend."

He tried to touch her, but she moved back and held up a hand, warning him to stop. He blew out a sharp breath. "The business meeting was with her and our banker."

"*Our?*"

"Laurel, don't," he warned, bringing a fresh load of tears to her eyes.

"Don't what, Charlie? Expect truth and honesty? Because I can't be in a relationship without that."

"I didn't lie—"

"You didn't tell the truth. Same thing."

He slowly shook his head. "I didn't want to hurt you or make you worry."

"And this isn't?" She jerked the back of her hand to her mouth to prevent a sob from escaping, but it was too late. She was raw, open, and bleeding tears right in front of him. "You need to go."

"No. Not until you listen."

She sucked in a shaky breath. "There's nothing you can say, Charlie. You lied about where you were last weekend and who you were with. I need to be with someone I can trust."

"Fuck." He tossed the word to the ground like it was a venomous spider. "I love you, Laurel. The reason I didn't tell you is that it was no big deal. I needed to sign paperwork, and she asked me to stay for her celebration. I didn't say anything to you because I didn't want you to think it was something it wasn't."

She drew a hand across her cheek, wiping at her tears. "What kind of paperwork?"

He closed his eyes and whispered, "For a loan."

She hiccupped on a sob. "Oh, God. This just gets worse."

"It was to replace a larger loan, Laurel. Smaller amount, better interest rates. It worked out better for both of us. Dammit, Laurel. Siobhan and I have been friends for a long time. She helped me through some rough times, and I've done the same for her. That's all there is to it. Nothing more."

Yet he'd never mentioned Siobhan to her. God, how she wished she could believe him. "Please go."

He held out his hands toward her, palms up. "Laurel..."

Her heart wavered, and her mind threw a powder keg of raw emotion on top of it. "Get out." Her voice grew stronger. "Now. Get the hell off my property and the hell out of my life."

She slammed the door in his face and crumpled to the ground on the other side. When he wouldn't leave, she crawled across the floor until she reached her bedroom. From there, she found her way back into bed and pulled her quilt tightly around her as sobs worked to purge brutal pain from her soul.

She couldn't do this. Not anymore.

Her heart couldn't take it.

She'd go back to the way things were before Charlie. Quiet and safe. Focused on work. Those things made her happy.

This? *This* was all an illusion. Something she'd wanted to be true so she could have a love like Afton.

From now on, when the loneliness became too much, she'd

jump off a cliff or hurl herself at break-neck speeds down a mountainside.

She might crash and burn, but she could heal from those injuries. She was quite certain she'd never get over this.

22

Hours later, Laurel pulled herself from her bed, in fear of losing her mind. She'd staunched her tears for the moment, though the pain boiled in her heart like an angry volcano.

She ached to call Afton, the one friend who'd always been there for her. But Afton was biased, and it would be completely unfair of Laurel to put her in the middle of this. She knew, if forced, Afton would choose her, but that would mess up everything in her life as well.

One messed up life was enough.

Raw and barely functioning, she dressed, threw on her hiking shoes, and leashed up Jasper. She needed air and trees. Jasper could handle the canyon trail just outside Aspen for a little while before he'd tire. If she couldn't bear to come home after that, then they'd rest together or maybe play in the trees. She grabbed a tennis ball and stuffed it into her backpack before she headed out.

Jasper barked and danced around her, excited to be going. His leash always meant fun. As she turned to close the door behind her, she caught sight of an envelope taped to her door.

Her heart lurched. The envelope taunted her as her mind puzzled through how to handle it. She knew it was from Charlie. She hadn't been willing to listen to him, so he'd figured out another way to keep feeding her lies.

As much as she ached for any connection with him, she knew she shouldn't. If she didn't open it, he couldn't lie to her again. He could only enter her safe bubble if she let him.

God, she was a mess.

She snatched it off the door, marched to the outside trash can and threw it in before she headed to her Jeep. "Come on, Jasper." She picked up the squirming pup and placed him in the passenger seat. He jumped and succeeded in placing two wet, sloppy kisses before she could move out of the way.

An unexpected chuckle escaped her lips as she closed the door behind him. Then the fact that she had shown happiness drew another ache from deep inside her. How could she laugh when her heart was so completely shattered? Tears formed in her eyes, and she worked furiously to blink them away.

Damn him. Why her? Why couldn't Charlie have left her alone like she'd asked?

She squeezed her eyes shut as a fresh wave of anguish rolled over her.

"Ugh," she yelled toward the sky. "Damn him!"

Instead of climbing into her Jeep, she strode back to the trash, pulled out his letter, and pushed it to the bottom of her backpack. She'd burn it at a campsite along the trail. That way, she couldn't be tempted to read it later when she was feeling weak.

She fought her emotions as she drove, and by the time they reached the trailhead, she'd pieced herself back together. Somewhat. As best as she could at that moment. In the past, her counselor had said that was all that counted.

They walked until Jasper finally stopped and plopped on

the ground, his way of saying they'd gone far enough. She picked him up and tossed him over her shoulder as she headed for the closest campsite to rest.

Poor pup. He didn't deserve to be stressed because of her issues. But she needed him near her. Needed to know that another living being loved her and wouldn't let her down.

Once she reached the campsite, she tied Jasper to the picnic table just in case he had a sudden burst of energy, and she sat next to him. She drank water from a bottle she found in her pack from a previous hike. Weeks old and stale, but she didn't care. She poured some into her hand for Jasper. He lapped it up and then promptly laid down in the nearby grass and closed his eyes.

She tilted her face heavenward and closed hers as well. The softest of breezes caressed her cheeks. Hints of sunlight filtered through the trees and flashed behind her eyelids. She focused on her breathing as nature soothed her soul.

She had to burn it. She had to.

Reluctantly, she opened her eyes and stared sideways at her pack. She was a stronger person now than she'd been in the past. She couldn't let this pain own her, not like she had with Abercrombie.

This was her life, goddammit. *Hers.*

With determination, she pulled the lighter from a front pocket and then dug for Charlie's letter. By the time she wrangled it out from beneath a wadded jacket and other things, the envelope was crumpled, no longer fresh and smooth.

She moved to the fire pit and crouched. With a flick, the lighter produced a small flame, and she held the envelope over it.

It smoked, and she panicked, dropping the envelope to the ground before it could catch fire.

"Dammit!" she yelled and then picked up the envelope. She

closed her eyes while her heart battled her mind. She blinked back several tears and exhaled a shaky, but not broken breath before she returned to the picnic table.

Cursing her weakness, she slid her finger beneath the flap as she sat and then pulled out a piece of lined notebook paper covered with his writing.

Laurel, please don't shatter our hearts like this. I love you. I've loved you from the moment I saw you. There isn't and never will be another woman for me.

Her heart quivered as she fought to contain her tears.

Siobhan is only a friend. Yes, she's a good friend, but there's nothing more between us, hasn't been for years. I didn't mention her because I was afraid if I did, you'd think badly of me or get angry. Then you wouldn't feel safe giving me your heart, and you'd leave. Please don't leave me.

You told me you needed someone safe, and I've worked hard to give you that peace. I kept something from you that I shouldn't have, and I can see now that by trying to protect you, I've broken your trust.

You can't imagine the pain that brings me. I will never forgive myself if I've fucked up the most important thing in my life.

Please talk to me, Laurel. Give me a chance. Look in my eyes one last time and tell me your future isn't there, too. One chance. Just give me one.

I love you with everything I have and everything that I am. Charlie

Laurel inhaled a shaky breath and realized tears streamed down her cheeks. He'd used those pretty words before, and she'd given him her whole heart. What a fool.

This time, when she returned to the fire pit, she had no problem lighting his letter and watching it burn. She wished she could do the same with her heart.

Leaves in the trees above fluttered, but she found no peace there, like she'd hoped.

She gathered her tired pup and backpack and headed down the trail. She'd go home and sleep. Maybe for days. She'd cling to anything that would help time pass until she could breathe again.

At the turn into her driveway, she spotted Charlie's truck in front of her house. She slammed on her brakes and pounded angry fists on her steering wheel. Why couldn't he leave her alone? He knew what he'd done and couldn't pretend otherwise. If she could stand the sight of him, she'd ask him why he had to be so cruel. But not now. Not today.

She pressed on her accelerator again and drove away. Minutes later, she found herself at the only place she had left to go.

Her mom opened the door, took one look at her, and Laurel burst into tears.

Joanna opened her arms. "Oh, honey. Come here."

Laurel fell into her embrace as a fresh wave of sobs pulled her under. Her mom dragged her farther into the house and sat her on the couch next to her. She pulled several tissues from a box near her lamp and closed Laurel's fingers around them.

Her mom held her as she cleansed what she could from her soul. "It's okay, baby. You go ahead and cry."

At least she could cry now. For months after Abercrombie, she'd shown nothing but stone-cold emotions.

Her mother stroked her hair, soothing her. "Charlie was here earlier," she whispered.

Laurel sat up and faced her mother. "What? No."

Her mom took her hand and squeezed. "It's okay."

"It's not okay. None of this is okay."

"He's as messed up as you are. He told me what happened—"

She lifted a hand between them. "Did he tell you he spent the weekend with his girlfriend?" Probably not.

"Yes, he did. Not the weekend, but that he'd visited a friend he'd once dated without telling you."

"He lied about her. Never mentioned a word to me."

Her mom pulled her back into her embrace. "I know."

Laurel worked to control her breathing as they both sat silently on the couch. "Why aren't you angry at him?" she finally asked. Her mother had always been the first to come to her defense. "He hurt me."

"He didn't mean to hurt you. He acted on a bad decision when he shouldn't have."

She sat up again to face her mother, not understanding her reaction at all. "How can you believe him?"

Her expression grew gentle with care and concern. "I've been around many people during my lifetime, and I think I've grown to be a decent judge of character."

"We don't trust people," she countered.

"We haven't in the past. But Laurel, honey, that boy loves you. I couldn't deny it if I wanted to. I didn't want you to date, didn't want any of this to happen. But it's made me realize sheltering you from life never protected you. When I watched you two at the wedding, I realized my mistake."

She narrowed her gaze and sniffed. "You watched us?"

"Of course, I watched you. You were the most beautiful woman in the room. Charlie never took his eyes off you, either. He told me he loves you. I don't know if you want to hear this, but I believe he does. He didn't tell you about his friend because he didn't want to scare you away."

"He lied."

She slowly shook her head. "He made a very poor choice, but he does love you. With all his heart, I believe. If you love him, too, you need to work this out. Men like him don't come around often."

She couldn't believe what she heard. Her mother wanted her to forgive him? That hadn't been in her realm of possibilities a few moments ago, but now?

Her mom patted her hand. "Give him a chance to explain. Put aside everything that's happened in your past and judge him by what you see in his eyes and in his heart."

She inhaled a shaky breath. "I don't know if I can."

"Yes, you can. You've made it through much worse. You can do this. For you, Laurel. You deserve to be happy."

She closed her eyes for a long moment and breathed. She tucked away her emotions and focused on the facts. She'd honestly believed he loved her and that the connection she'd shared with him was real.

It had seemed so damned real.

What if it was? What if he had made an extremely dumb mistake but hadn't cheated on her?

The idea sparked hope inside her. She refused to fan the flame. But she realized she needed to see him again. Needed to hear him out. If her mother, who never wanted to see her with anyone, believed he loved her...

Laurel had to know.

She had to do what he'd asked, had to look him in the eye with her mind clear.

She'd always been able to trust her instincts, and she had to trust that she'd know what was right for her and what wasn't. She'd listen with an open heart, and she'd know.

With that thought in mind, she said goodbye to her mother. She carried Jasper back to her Jeep and headed straight for Charlie's house. At his porch, she hesitated, wondering if she should knock or walk in. Before she could choose, the door opened. Charlie didn't speak as he scooped her into his arms.

Emotion shook his chest and brought her tears to the surface again.

He held her for a long time, and she didn't try to escape. She realized she didn't need to face him down with questions to know the truth. This was the truth. This man loved her with all his heart, just like she did him.

"I'm sorry." Her apology came out in a broken whisper.

"You're sorry?" He pulled back and searched her face. Tears wet his eyelashes, too. "I'm the one who's sorry."

She sniffed and shook her head. "I should have listened to you. I should have trusted."

He cupped her face in his hands. "I should have trusted you, too. I struggle sometimes to remember that you've grown stronger and those things you told me are far in the past. But I want to protect you from everything and everyone."

She smiled through her tears. "You can't."

"I know. But I can love you through whatever life brings. Let me do that, Laurel. Let me love you."

Her throat tightened and blocked her words, so she nodded instead.

He crushed her against him. "This is right, Laurel."

"Yes," she managed. "This is right where I want to be. Forever."

EPILOGUE

Laurel sat in the shade behind her house with a book propped in her lap. Jasper lay at her feet, snoozing. Over the last month, he'd grown much bigger, and every day he looked less and less like a puppy. He could keep up with her on the trails now, but he'd always be her sweet baby.

The sound of several yaps drew her attention, and Jasper jumped to attention. Five little golden lab pups tumbled over each other near the corner of the house, barking and biting each other in their play.

She sighed and stood, wondering how they'd gotten out of their enclosure. Thank God none had gotten lost along the way. As she crossed the lawn, she realized each had a rolled piece of paper tucked into its collar. She narrowed her gaze as a smile curved her lips, and she searched the perimeter.

Somebody was up to something.

As she approached, they caught sight of her and bounded toward her. When they met, she dropped into the cool grass next to them. They barked and climbed, trying to reach her face. She laughed as she slipped the papers from each of them.

Once again, she looked for signs of Charlie, but he'd made himself scarce.

She unrolled the first one. In big block letters, he'd written *me*.

Her grin grew bigger. The next was a question mark. Another said *you*.

She opened the next, found *marry*, and her heart stalled. The last said, *will*.

Will you marry me?

She looked up to see the puppies' mama trotting across the grass toward her. She also had something tied to her neck. A pouch. With something square inside.

"Come here, Matilda." She patted her leg, and the dog hurried faster. Laurel got to her knees and then untied the package from Matilda's collar. She slipped the box from the pouch and opened it.

Her breath caught in her throat at the sight of the glittering square-cut diamond, and she sat back on the grass, stunned.

"Will you marry me?" Charlie's voice came from behind her, and she turned with a startle.

A wide smile curved his lips as mischief danced in his eyes. He chuckled as she jumped to her feet and hurried toward him. He caught her with a fierce hug and twirled her around, her emotions spinning in delighted circles as well. With her heart thudding, she held onto him for a long moment after he set her back on her feet.

Grinning, he took the box from her hand, and she shivered as he pulled the ring from the setting. Instead of handing it to her, he knelt before her, with love shimmering in his eyes.

She placed her hand over her heart, unable to contain her happiness. They'd come a long way from their first date. She'd almost missed out on this incredibly sweet moment because she'd been scared.

Love shone in his eyes as he focused on her. "Laurel, will you do me the greatest honor of becoming my wife? I promise to love and cherish you forever."

She'd found her strong, safe, and steady man. The one she could love for the rest of her life. "Yes," she said as happy tears sprang to her eyes.

He stood and slid the sparkling ring on her finger before he kissed her senseless. When they finished, she stared into the eyes of the man she loved. "This will be the greatest, happiest adventure of my life. We'll have babies and puppies and kitties, and so much love."

He chuckled. "Yes. That and so much more."

————

I hope you enjoyed Laurel and Charlie's love story. Sign up for my newsletter to receive notifications of new releases, freebies, and special sales at www.CindyStark.com. Also, if you have a moment, I'd appreciate a review!

Thank you very much, and happy reading!
Cindy

ABOUT THE AUTHOR

Award-winning author Cindy Stark lives in a small town shadowed by the Rocky Mountains. She enjoys writing about forever love with hot men and strong women in her sexy contemporary romances, along with penning unexpected twists in her emotional romantic suspense stories, and creating magical mayhem in her paranormal cozy mysteries.

She'd like to think she's the boss of her three adorable and sassy cats, but deep down, she knows she's ruled by kitty overlords. Someday, she hopes to earn enough to open a cat sanctuary where she can save all the kitties and play all day with toe beans and murder mittens.

Connect with her online at
www.CindyStark.com

ALSO BY CINDY STARK

ASPEN SERIES (Small Town Sexy Romance):

Wounded (Prequel)

Relentless

Lawless

Cowboys and Angels

Come Back To Me

Surrender

Reckless

Tempted

Crazy One More Time

I'm With You

Breathless

PINECONE VALLEY (Small Town Sexy Romance):

Love Me Again

Love Me Always

ARGENT SPRINGS (Small Town Sexy Romance):

Whispers

Secrets

BLACKWATER CANYON RANCH (Western Sexy Romance):

Caleb

Oliver

Justin

Piper

Jesse

RETRIBUTION NOVELS (Sexy Romantic Suspense):

Branded

Hunted

Banished

Hijacked

Betrayed

COOKIE CORNER COZY MYSTERIES (PG-Rated Fun):

Cookie Calamity

Haunted Cookies

Cursed Cookies

Conjured Cookies

Killer Cookies

Shadow Cookies

SWEET MOUNTAIN WITCHES COZY MYSTERIES (PG-Rated Fun):

Midlife or Death

For Once in My Midlife

One Midlife to Live

Midlife in the Fast Lane

Midlife of the Party

Such is Midlife

Mysterious Midlife

Love of my Midlife

Merry Midlife

CRYSTAL COVE COZY MYSTERIES (PG-Rated Fun):

Murder and Moonstones

Brews and Bloodstone

Curses and Carnelian

Killer Kyanite

Rumors and Rose Quartz

Hexes and Hematite

TEAS & TEMPTATIONS COZY MYSTERIES (PG-Rated Fun):

Once Wicked

Twice Hexed

Three Times Charmed

Four Warned

The Fifth Curse

It's All Sixes

Spellbound Seven

Elemental Eight

Nefarious Nine

Hijacked Honeymoon

A Witch Without a Spell

Mystical Mayhem

WITCHES OF PORT TOWNSEND (Sexy Paranormal Romance):

Which Witch is Which

Which Witch is Wicked

Which Witch is Wild

Which Witch is Willing

OTHER TITLES:

Sweet Vengeance

<u>Moonlight and Margaritas</u>

www.ingramcontent.com/pod-product-compliance
Lightning Source LLC
Chambersburg PA
CBHW020149120726
47903CB00007B/2467